V

X

"God, woman, you do turn me inside out. You always have."

"I'm sorry. I didn't mean to send mixed signals—" Alaina stammered.

He traced her lips. "You turning me inside out has always been a good thing. We may have argued about a lot of issues, but we always connected on a physical level. I meant it when I said I wouldn't pressure you to take this faster than you're ready."

"That's good to know. The attraction between us is…problematic."

"We were married for years. Even if your brain doesn't remember, I believe that on some level your body does. We'll just take things slow until your mind catches up."

He offered her another piece of dark chocolate. Her fingertips gingerly brushed his as she took it. Another confusing jolt of desire burst through her.

"What if my mind doesn't ever catch up?"

A devilish smile spread across his lips. "Then we'll start over."

A Christmas Baby Surprise

CATHERINE MANN

MILLS
BOON®

First published in Great Britain 2015
by Mills & Boon, an imprint of Harlequin (UK) Limited,
Large Print edition 2015
Eton House, 18-24 Paradise Road,
Richmond, Surrey, TW9 1SR

© 2015 Catherine Mann

ISBN: 978-0-263-26049-6

Harlequin (UK) Limited's policy is to use papers that
are natural, renewable and recyclable products and made
from wood grown in sustainable forests. The logging
and manufacturing processes conform to the legal
environmental regulations of the country of origin.

Printed and bound in Great Britain
by CPI Antony Rowe, Chippenham, Wiltshire

USA TODAY bestselling author **Catherine Mann** lives on a sunny Florida beach with her flyboy husband and their four children. With more than forty books in print in over twenty countries, she has also celebrated wins for both a RITA® Award and a Booksellers' Best Award. Catherine enjoys chatting with readers online— thanks to the wonders of the internet, which allows her to network with her laptop by the water! Contact Catherine through her website, catherinemann.com, find her on Facebook and Twitter (@CatherineMann1), or reach her by snail mail at PO Box 6065, Navarre, FL 32566.

To my awesome editor Stacy Boyd!

One

Alaina Rutger was living her childhood dream—a family of her own. Her charismatic husband was driving her home from the hospital with their infant son strapped into a car seat. She had the perfect life.

If only she could remember the man who'd put the four-carat diamond wedding ring on her finger.

A man who called himself Porter Rutger. Husband. Father of her child. And a man who'd been wiped from her memory along with the past five years of her life.

She tore her eyes away from his broad shoulders and coal-dark hair as she sat in back with their baby. Her baby. Alaina tucked the monogrammed red blanket over the infant as he slept, one foot in a booty, the other in a cast that had begun the repair on his clubfoot.

Another person she didn't remember. Another heartbreak in her upside-down world. A week ago, she'd woken in the hospital with no memory of the man sitting by her bedside or of the blue bundle in the bassinet.

Waking up from a coma had felt a lot like coming to after the worst hangover ever, her head throbbing so badly she could barely move. But a quick look around showed her a hospital room rather than a bedroom.

And a hot man sleeping in the chair, his dark hair rumpled. His black pants and white button-down wrinkled.

Her own Doctor McDreamy?

"Hello," she'd croaked out, her throat raw for a sip of water.

McDreamy bolted awake quickly. "Alaina?" He blinked, scrubbed his hand across his eyes in disbelief, then shot to his feet. "Oh, God, you're awake. I need to get the nurse."

"Water," she rasped out. "Please, a drink."

He thumbed the nurses' call button. "I don't know what the doctors will want. Maybe ice chips. Your IV has been feeding you. Soon, though, I promise, whatever you want, soon."

The nurses? Doctors? He wasn't Doc Mc-Dreamy? Then... "Who are you?"

He looked up from the control panel of buttons slowly, his eyes wide with disbelief. "Who am I?"

She pressed her fingertips to her monster headache. "I'm sorry, but I feel like hell. What happened?"

"Alaina..." He sank slowly into the chair, his voice measured, guarded. "We were in a car accident."

"We?" She knew him?

"Yes," he said, leaning closer to cover her hand carefully. "Alaina, my name's Porter and I'm your husband."

The shock of that revelation still echoed through her.

Once the nurse and doctor had checked her over Porter had further explained they'd been in a car wreck a month prior, after picking up little Thomas from the adoption agency. Her husband… Porter. Porter Rutger. God, she still struggled to remember his name. Porter told her the baby had a birth defect and had spent the past month going through surgeries while she'd been in a coma from the accident.

Too soon, before she felt ready to handle this life she'd landed in, it was time to leave the hospital. She'd been told many first moms felt that way.

But not all new mothers had amnesia.

Her throat burned with bile and fears that hadn't abated since she'd woken from the coma a week ago thinking it was November, only to find it was December.

Five years later.

Five years of memories simply gone, pushed out of her head in the course of a month. Most devastating, she'd lost the four and a half years Porter had been in her life.

How was it that four weeks asleep could steal so much of her life? That coma had left her mind missing a substantial chunk of memories and yet her body felt 100 percent normal. She'd even been attracted to her stranger husband, so attracted that the aches and lethargy left over from her coma hadn't dulled the shiver of awareness she'd felt at the brush of his hands against her as he helped her from the hospital bed and into the car.

She swallowed hard and turned to look out the window at the rolling waves as the Mercedes traveled the Florida coastal road toward what Porter had told her was their beach mansion. They also owned a home in Tallahassee but they'd been closer to the beach home when picking up the baby, then having the wreck. Traveling with their infant son so fresh from surgery and her so recently out of a coma hadn't seemed wise. The doctors had advised they stay close for the short term at least.

Porter had quickly suggested they stay at their nearby vacation home. Apparently her tall, dark and studly husband was wealthier than Midas, thanks to his construction empire that won major contracts to build corporate structures around the country. They had no financial worries as she recovered, he'd told her. Another reason to be grateful.

But instead of gratitude, she could only feel fear at the imbalance of power between her and this man who was her husband. She was adrift with only the facts he told her about her past. No family since her parents were dead. No friends, other than people she apparently hadn't seen in five years, since her breakup from an abusive boyfriend. She'd cut herself off from everyone then.

Still, she was missing the months following that breakup, the months leading up to her meeting Porter. Falling in love with him. Marrying him. He said after they married, they'd moved to southeastern Florida, away from her hometown in North Carolina. She believed what he said, but wondered what parts he might not have mentioned. Men could be so brief in their explanations, leaving out details or emotional components a woman would find crucial.

Porter glanced in the rearview mirror, his brown eyes as dark as undiluted coffee full of caffeinated energy.

Jolt.

"Alaina, is everything all right?" he said, his Southern drawl muted by some experience in another region.

Something else she didn't know about him unless he told her.

What kind of answer did he expect from her? More of the same dodgy responses they'd given each other over the past week since she woke up? Guarded words spoken in front of doctors or said out of fear her fragile world might shatter into a somnolent fog again?

Each mile closer to a vacation home she couldn't recall stretched the tension inside her tighter until she snapped softly, "Did the doctor give you any more insight as to why can't I remember the past five years? Nearly a quarter of my life is just gone."

"The doctor spoke with you. He has an obligation to be honest with you. You're his patient." The man in the front seat who called himself her husband was unfailingly polite but lacked the kind of warmth that Alaina would have envisioned in a man she'd married.

Her husband.

What had made her choose this coolly controlled male for a mate? Another question she couldn't begin to answer. In spite of the spark that seemed to arc between them amidst the questions.

"I haven't forgotten that conversation. It was more of a rhetorical question because there are so many other things I don't understand." She glanced down at her sleeping son in his impossibly cute elf pajamas. "Such as, how could anyone forget a child this precious?"

Her heart swelled to look at Thomas, his tiny nose and Cupid's-bow mouth calling to her every maternal instinct. She'd always wanted children, dreamed of having a big family after growing up an only child. If she and Porter had been married for almost four years, what had made them wait to start their family?

"You'd only known him for a couple of hours before the accident." Porter turned onto a secluded drive where mammoth houses were hidden by manicured privacy hedges on one side, although she knew the other side opened to the water.

"The length of time shouldn't matter. He's a child, my child—" she paused, brushing her fingers across the top of an impossibly small and soft hand "—our child. That's life changing. A minute. An hour. A couple of hours. That should be burned in here." She tapped the front of her head.

"Even if your marriage wasn't?" he asked wryly.

Contrition nipped. This had to be tough for him, too. "I'm sorry. This can't be easy for you, either."

"You're alive and awake, more than I ever

expected to have again." He said the emotional words with a harsh rasp as he guided the car along the palm tree–lined road. "I can deal with the rest."

"You make me feel as if I shouldn't be frustrated."

"Give yourself time." He kept both hands on the wheel, the late-day sunshine glinting off his Patek Philippe wristwatch. "You've been through a lot."

How did she know the brand of his watch but not know if the band on his ring finger had an inscription? But then, she remembered studying art history when she'd got her bachelor's degree. Recalled a love of finely made things and beautiful objects. Maybe that was why the watch resonated and the ring…nothing.

"What about you? What have you been through this past month? It must have been horrible, with a child in surgery and a wife in a coma."

"That doesn't matter," he said, his voice clipped. "I'm fine now."

Her mouth twitched with amusement as the car braked at a stop sign wrapped in garland. "Are you one of those men who's too tough to be vulnerable?"

His eyes met hers solemnly in the mirror. "I'm a man who thought he'd lost everything."

And just that fast, she felt her terrified heart melt a little for this stranger husband of hers. "You still have, in a way," she said sympathetically, "because of me and how I've lost any sense of us and our memories."

At the deserted intersection, he twisted to look over the seat at her, his elbow resting along the back and tugging his button-down shirt across his muscular chest. "You and our son are alive. That truly is what's most important to me."

There had been tension between them since she'd woken up in the hospital. He still held all the answers she couldn't access. But now, with the sincerity shining in his eyes, she wanted to hug him, ached to wrap her arms around him and have him do the same to her. Most of all, to have that feel familiar. She stretched a hand out to touch his elbow lightly—

A car honked behind them and she jerked her hand back. What was she thinking? Except for the few things he'd told her, she knew nothing about him or her or what kind of life they'd built together. Or what kind of future they might have because these events had changed them. Undoubtedly.

However for Thomas, she and Porter had to try for a level of peace between them. Could the Christmas spirit work a miracle for her family?

Shifting nervously in her seat, Alaina toyed with the reindeer baby rattle, gathering up her rapidly fraying nerve. "May I ask you questions about the past?"

"Why didn't you question more before?" He kept his eyes on the road this time.

In some ways maybe that made this conversation easier.

"Because…I was scared you wouldn't answer."

"What's changed?"

"We're not in the hospital. There are no doctors who make me do all the work thinking, insisting I should only remember what I'm ready to know. They kept asking me not to push to remember, but that's causing me even more stress, wondering." She needed to know. How could she be a real wife to Porter and a mother to Thomas if she didn't even know who she was or how they'd become a family?

"You trust me to answer truthfully?" He glanced back at her, his eyes darkening.

"What do you have to gain by lying?"

Now wasn't that a loaded question? One that called for total trust in a man she barely knew. But she had no other choice, not if she wanted to reconnect as a family. "How did we meet?"

"My firm was handling building an addition to a museum where you worked. You saw me flex my muscles and here we are."

He sure did have muscles, and if they'd enticed her half as much then as they did now she could see how he would have caught her attention. His humor made him even more appealing. "You're funny, after all, Porter."

"You think I don't have a sense of humor? You've wounded my ego."

"There hasn't been a lot of room for levity this week." She'd been so damn scared in the hospital. Walking the halls at night when she couldn't sleep. Obsessively checking on the baby and praying she would remember something, anything from the past five years.

Most of all, wondering about the mysterious, handsome man who'd spent hours with her each day.

"True enough. Hopefully we can fix that. We have the whole holiday season to relax, settle our child and get to know each other again." Through the rearview mirror, he held her eyes with a determined intensity. "Because, make no mistake, I intend to remind you of all the reasons we fell in love in the first place."

His words made something go hot inside her, a mixture of desire and confusion and, yes, nerves. She swallowed hard. It didn't help. But even if she didn't remember it, this was her life. There was no choice but to push on. To regain her memories and her life.

And figure out just what this man—her husband—meant to her. Not just in the past. But now.

Porter Rutger had been through hell.

But for the first time in a long time he saw a way to climb back out.

His hands clenched the steering wheel as he drove his wife and son home from the hospital. The past month—worrying about how Thomas would recover from his first surgery for his clubfoot, wondering about possible hidden effects of the accident on the baby…

And all the while his wife had been in a coma.

Porter's jaw flexed as he studied the familiar beach road leading to the vacation home they'd chosen after their third in vitro failed. Before they'd adopted Thomas, their marriage had showed signs of fraying from years of struggling with the stresses of infertility.

He and Alaina had been in hell for a long time, even before the accident. He'd thought they'd hit rock bottom when they'd contacted a divorce attorney. They'd been so close to signing the divorce papers when the call came about a baby to adopt. A special-needs baby, difficult to place, an infant who required surgeries and years of physical therapy. While foster care would have provided the basics, the search for a home would have to start all over again if they backed out, leaving the baby adrift in the system.

They hadn't made the decision to adopt on a whim. They'd started the adoption process two years ago when the reality of infertility had become clear. Then they'd faced more heartache waiting. Their already strained marriage hadn't fared well under the added stress.

To this day, he couldn't remember which of them had asked for a divorce. The words had been thrown out during an argument and then taken root, growing fast, lawyers involved. It had damn near torn him apart, but their constant arguments had made it impossible to envision a future together bringing up the family they both wanted so much. Even marriage counseling hadn't helped.

They'd reached the end—and then the call had come about Thomas.

He and Alaina had put their differences aside to adopt the baby and stay together temporarily. Her soft, open heart had welcomed the baby from the second the call had come. Thomas needed them. That had cinched the deal for Alaina.

Then the accident happened and the possibility of losing her completely had made him want to shred the documents. Maybe he could have that family he wanted after all.

And he'd had no idea how quickly that little bundle in the back would steal his heart. He would do anything for his son. Anything.

While he would also do anything to have Alaina healthy, he couldn't ignore the fact that he had a second chance to win her over—for himself and for their son. This could be a fresh start, a way to work through all the pain they'd caused each other in the past.

Yes, he'd made mistakes in their marriage, but this was a new opportunity to build the family he'd always wanted. Growing up with a single-mom lawyer who worked all the time and husband-hunted during her hours off, he'd craved stability, love.

If he could only gain Alaina's forgiveness, or convince her that he was in it for the long haul this time, that he'd changed. Hell, if he could just make Alaina realize he wasn't the man he'd been a few weeks ago, then he could have the family he'd always dreamed of. The one they'd both wanted.

He'd never been one to procrastinate or waste time. He was a man of action.

And the stakes had never been more important than now.

Porter glanced in the rearview mirror at his blonde wife, the woman he'd fallen head over heels in love with four and a half years ago. Her intelligence, confidence and artistic flair had mesmerized him. He'd seen her discussing gallery art with a visiting class of elementary school students and he'd known. She was the one. She was his every perfect fantasy—soft, openhearted. He could envision her cradling their babies. Making sand castles with toddlers. Painting with children.

And it hadn't been just the maternal images that drew him. She had a passionate nature that set him on fire. Even now, the memories turned him inside out.

But the more they'd argued, the more he'd realized how shaky their foundation had been.

"What did you want to know?"

"We didn't talk much at all in the hospital." Her blue eyes held his for an electric instant before she looked away.

"The doctor's orders. And things were hectic, with Thomas's physical therapists and your tests." He'd been pulled in two different directions even though he'd taken time off from work, passing over control of his construction firm to his second in command until he had his family in order. Seeing her so helpless in the hospital had sucker punched him. Their love for each other might have died, but they still shared a history, an attraction, and now a child. His need for the picture-perfect family had destroyed their marriage and their love for each other.

But he owed it to her to take care of her while she healed and while they figured out how to parent Thomas.

"I'm not blaming anyone," she said quickly. "I'm just trying to fill in the blanks so I can function. I felt so…limited in the hospital."

He wouldn't sabotage her recovery. The doctors had said she shouldn't push to remember, and he planned to honor that directive. He wasn't that ruthless, no matter what his competitors said. But he sure as hell wasn't going to squander this chance to convince her to stay.

He would do whatever it took to keep her in this family. He wasn't interested in being a part-time father, and had never been, even when he'd agreed to sign those damn divorce papers. He'd regretted that decision the moment he'd made it. How could he have the family he needed if he let his wife walk away? Even then, regardless of their problems, he'd wanted things to go back to the way they'd been in the beginning.

He didn't know what had gone wrong, what more she expected of him. And now that she couldn't remember their life together, he might not ever find out. "The doctor wanted to see how much you recalled on your own. We didn't want you to confuse memories with things you'd been told."

"Maybe hearing about us might help jog those memories."

He noticed she didn't mention the whole trust issue again. Did that mean she'd put it on the back burner? Or she was willing to take him at his word?

She sure as hell hadn't trusted him at the end of their marriage, before the accident. Would that distrust eek through even her thick fog of amnesia? He steered off the highway onto the access road to their security gate.

"Porter, I don't have a choice but to ask you these questions. There's no one else from my past I still have a relationship with. If I want to find out anything about these past five years, it's you or Google."

He chuckled darkly. "A ringing endorsement if ever I heard one."

A smile played with her full lips. It was almost comfortable and it caused his chest to tighten. He remembered a time when he'd been able to make her smile every day, back before their relationship had deteriorated into loud fights and long silences.

"Porter, I'm not going to apologize for speaking the truth." The smile faded. "Why didn't anyone come see me in the hospital?"

"When the accident happened, we were far from home, picking up the baby. Our friends weren't nearby." And no doubt they would have felt awkward coming to visit the couple given the impending divorce. "I saved the cards from the flowers and balloons that came at the start. I'll show you when we get home."

She chewed that full lip. "What about phone calls to quiz people? Who can I call to help me?"

He wouldn't isolate her, but he didn't want to make it easy for her to take off again, either. He just wanted a little time for them to cement their relationship again, to rediscover what they'd once had—and to parent the baby they'd always wanted. They needed this time to become the family he'd always imagined they could be.

"The doctor warned you to be careful and take it slow. You'll have to ask your physicians near the beach house. Whatever they say is good by me." It surprised him that she hadn't asked many questions publicly at the hospital, but whatever had held her back, now that they were alone, she was more relentless about getting answers. There was an urgency and an edge to her now that she hadn't possessed before the accident.

Or had she kept it hidden the way she'd hidden so many of her motives in the last months of their marriage?

"So you have no trouble giving me those phone numbers? If the doctor says it's okay." She leaned forward, resting her arms on the back of the seat as they waited at an intersection.

"No problem at all." People would be eager to hear from her after the accident, but they'd also be busy with the holidays. And the doctor had given them no reason to think her memory would return so soon. He needed the next two weeks' Christmas holiday with her and their son to tell her his side of the story. To see if they could make this work. Maybe, just maybe they could build that family after all. For Thomas. "Whatever you want from me, just ask. We're married."

Her quick gasp brushed across his neck, and her gaze met his, her eyes wide. "Whatever I want?"

The air went hot between them. Could she see the memories in his eyes? Could she sense just how damn good they had been together? How good they could still be?

There was desire and apprehension in her eyes. Her gaze broadcast loud and clear that she might not share the same memories, but she felt their connection—and it made her nervous.

He needed to proceed carefully. He hadn't told her about their decision to divorce. He wanted the chance to convince her to stay first. He also didn't want her asking questions that would box him into lying—or telling a hard truth. Like the fact they hadn't slept together for a month before the accident. "I can promise you, I'm not about to demand husbandly rights or anything else from you until you're ready."

"That's for the best," she said a little too fast. "I'm not ready for—"

"You don't need to say anything more." He punched in the security code to open the scrolled gates that were designed like a pewter clamshell gaping wide. Christmas lights glistened on the palm trees lining the path to the yellow stucco mansion, the glimmer growing brighter with the setting sun.

"You've been very understanding the past

week, Porter. I know this has been difficult for you, too, and I appreciate that you've worked to make things as easy for me as possible."

There was a time not so long ago she'd made it clear she felt just the opposite. She'd insisted he only wanted her as a place holder in the mother role. That any woman would have done, that he didn't really love her and that she was damn well tired of him hiding at the office to avoid facing their problems.

He kept his silence.

"What? Did I say something wrong?"

"You've been through a lot the past month." They both had. He steered toward the three-story mansion perched on an ocean bluff, holi-day decor in full glory of wreaths, bows and draped garland as he'd ordered. "Of course you deserve understanding. I just want you to be clear that while I'm giving you time and space to remember your past, that doesn't mean I won't be trying to fill your head with happy new memories."

Her eyes went wide again. God, she was beautiful but too frail after all she'd been through. Protective urges fired to the fore. They might not be the couple they'd been before, but he needed her to make his family complete. He would do whatever it took to woo her over these next couple of weeks. And he wouldn't let anyone stand in his way.

He put the car in Park in front of the sweeping double staircase just as the groundskeeper stepped into another car to valet park…and…

Damn. Porter felt the sucker punch clear through to his spine.

He recognized that Maserati sports car well. Heaven help them all.

His mother had come to visit.

Two

Home sweet home?

Sorta.

Her eyes flitted to the sprawling house before them. Poinsettias lined the double staircase, adding Christmas spirit to the green and vibrant Florida winter. A giant wreath trimmed in gold and silver hung on the door, warm and inviting.

The warmth made her heart sink a bit. Had she picked out all of these decorations? Were they supposed to carry some sentimental value? She had been with Porter for almost five years. They owned years' worth of memories and items they had collected—and all of it was a mystery to her. Taking a deep breath, she turned her attention to Thomas and his monogrammed blanket.

As she unbuckled the baby from his car seat, Alaina couldn't miss the tension radiating from Porter. Of course he'd been under a tremendous stress, too, during this whole situation. He had just been so stalwart until now; she was surprised he let his emotions show.

Even if he'd opened up only briefly before he became the ultimate in-control guy again. Was that an act just for her? Was that how she'd preferred him to be? She'd liked seeing the emotion on his face, in his eyes. The controlled expression he wore now seemed to shut her out.

She cradled the sleeping infant in her arms, taking comfort from the scent of baby shampoo and innocence. She didn't remember becoming a wife or a mother. She didn't *feel* like a wife or a mother.

But she knew without question she would do whatever was needed to make sure this innocent life in her care felt loved and secure.

Porter opened the back door of the car, the setting sun casting a nimbus around his big body, which blocked out the rest of the world. God, he was a gorgeous hulk of man. She could see him in a painting of Atlas holding the world on those broad shoulders. He made her feel safe, protected. She could lean on him.

He propped a hand on the roof. "Are you feeling steady enough to carry the baby?"

"I'm fine, but thank you for asking." She stepped out, her hold careful on Thomas.

Porter cupped her elbow in a steadying grasp, his touch warm and gentle, sending tingles through her. She glanced at him quickly. Did he feel it, too? What was he thinking? He had to want his wife back. She wanted that for him, but even so, she couldn't shake the feeling that something was off between them. She couldn't miss how he only answered what was needed, never offering one snippet more. And his shoulders seemed so braced, tense. Where was the joy in this homecoming?

She straightened and adjusted her hold on the

baby. "Thank you. I really am okay to walk on my own."

It was strange how she'd been in a coma for a month and yet her body acted as if she'd simply taken a long nap. She'd spent a week doing physical therapy and eating high-nutrient meals to regain strength in her muscles. Other than tiring quickly, she felt no ill effects from her ordeal. At least not physically. How surreal.

"I'll get the car seat and diaper bag, then." He reached to lift them out, the navy blue Burberry bag looking tiny and incongruous in his large hands. "Before we step inside, I should warn you."

Foreboding gelled in her belly. Here it came. Whatever awful thing she'd feared her amnesia had been hiding from her. "Warn me about what?"

"My mother's here," he said with a heavy sigh.

She almost laughed in hysterical relief. She walked beside him toward the towering doors, inhaling a bracing breath of salty ocean breeze. "Your mom?" If he had a mother, why hadn't she come to the hospital? That seemed strange. She hadn't thought to question him about his family in the hospital since her memories stopped just before her relationship with Porter began. "You have a mother?"

"I wasn't born under a rock," he said with a sense of humor that still surprised her.

Another intriguing element to this man.

Chewing her bottom lip, Alaina eyed the door with trepidation. The gold and silver of the wreath caught in the amber sunset. "I wish you would have mentioned her arrival before now."

"I didn't know she was coming until I saw her car as we pulled up. It's very distinctive."

"Is your father here, too?"

"If so, that would be an even bigger surprise since I've never met the man."

"Oh, um, I'm sorry." Another thing about her husband she should have known.

"Thank you, but I'm long past looking for father figures around every corner. I'm looking forward to *being* a father." He reached to lift out the infant seat. "Let's go find out what coerced my mother to drive up from Miami."

Something about the way he said that made her sad, reminding her again of all the ways this should have been a happy day for him. His family was returning home from the hospital in good health. But she again felt that their life together—whatever it was now—couldn't be summed up that easily.

She wanted to trust him.

But something deep inside her, something beyond memory and born of instinct, held her back.

Luckily for him, his mother had been settling into her suite when he and Alaina brought Thomas into the house. His wife was in the nursery with their son now, which would give him a chance to talk to his mother alone first in his study. She needed to understand that he would toss her out on Christmas Day itself if she did one thing to upset this chance he had to win back his wife and keep his family intact.

He paced restlessly, his eyes drawn to the brass clock on his desk. What the hell was taking his mother so long? This wasn't the best of times for unexpected company, damn it.

Wooing Alaina back into his life and into his bed was going to be tough enough without having his mother throw verbal land mines into the mix with no warning. Courtney Rutger was a shark in the courtroom and in life. Their relationship had been strained since he'd walked out at eighteen and put himself through college working construction rather than take her money.

There were too many strings attached to his mother's gifts. The extravagant presents had clearly made Alaina uncomfortable given her less affluent upbringing and he couldn't blame her. Still, he'd never been quite sure how to navigate the tense waters between his mother and wife.

Finally, she glided into his study in a swirl of expensive perfume and one of her favored fitted Chanel suits. She leaned toward him for an air kiss on the cheek. "Porter."

He complied, as expected, wondering if she'd ever carried him around the way Alaina cradled Thomas. Making real contact, rather than an air kiss or half hug.

"Mom," he answered, angling away and leaning against his desk. "Why are you here?"

"To celebrate Christmas, and to help you with your new baby and your *wife*."

Help now? He wasn't buying it. His mother had visited only on holidays during his marriage, and she hadn't done more than come to the hospital the day after the accident. She'd seen her grandson, brought some gifts and flowers and left. She sure as hell hadn't cooed over her grandchild, much less snapped photos on her cell phone to share with her pals. "You've never been interested in babies before."

"I've never been a grandmother before."

"Mother…" He raised an eyebrow impatiently.

"Son," she answered with overplayed innocence.

"Is that what you're about? I'm your son. I know you. And you're not going to cause mother-in-law troubles."

"I don't know what you're talking about."

"Oh, Mother, please. You've made it clear for years that you don't like Alaina." The friction between his wife and mother, which had grown over time, had added pressure to an already strained marriage. "She's working to regain her memory and the last thing she needs is you tossing in digs or telling her things she's not ready to hear. She needs to be kept calm and happy while she recovers. She should remember the happy times first."

His gaze gravitated to the framed reproduction of a map of the Florida East Coast Railway from the Flagler Museum, an anniversary gift from Alaina two years ago. She'd respected his work, complimented him on being an artist in his own right through his construction company. She'd bought the gift in commemoration of another Florida builder/entrepreneur from the past.

Some people went on cruises for vacation. He and Alaina had spent their time off touring historic sites and discussing the architectural history of the buildings.

There had been good times between them… God, he missed what they'd once had.

And now he had a second chance. He wouldn't let anything or anyone stand in his way of repairing his relationship with Alaina. Of building a family together. It was too important.

"Your wife is ill now. I understand that and will be nice. If you're not ready for her to hear about the 'bad memories,' then okay. I'm here for all three of you." Courtney clicked her manicured nails. "I do have a heart."

She placed her hand dramatically on her chest, and gave a picture-perfect smile. It was with just such finesse that Courtney Rutger won over jury after jury—if not her son.

His mouth twitched with a smile. "That's questionable."

"And you're just like me." She winked. "Makes a mother proud."

He shook his head. "You're something else."

"That's one way to put it." She clapped her hands together. "Now where's my grandson?"

"He's getting his diaper changed."

Frowning, she smoothed back her French twist, her dark hair showing only a few threads of gray. "Then I'll wait a couple of minutes until he's through with that." She hesitated, shrugging. "What? I like to watch babies nap."

"Since when?"

"Since always. They're easier then." She grinned unrepentantly. "Now smile. It's the Christmas season. Your family is under one roof. And I certainly wouldn't have wagered a chance in hell on that happening this year."

Neither would he.

A creak of the door snapped his attention across the room. Alaina stood in the doorway frowning. Damn it. How much had she heard? Had his mother's strategic verbal land mines already blown his second chance all to hell? Courtney might have said she intended to respect his wishes, but he wasn't 100 percent certain she wouldn't try to find some way to finagle her way past on a technicality.

"Alaina?" he asked, waving her inside.

She stepped deeper into the room. "Please introduce me to your mother." She tugged a Christmas plaid burp cloth off the shoulder of her blue cotton dress that skimmed her curves. "I'm sorry I don't remember you, ma'am, but you're right. We're all lucky to be here together since I very well could have still been in that hospital bed. Or not here at all."

He exhaled hard, grateful she'd misunderstood his mother's comment. But he couldn't count on continued luck. He needed to make progress with his wife and get his family back. The sooner the better.

Two hours later, Alaina opened the closet in her bedroom. Hers and Porter's.

The space was larger than her first college studio apartment.

One side was lined with rows of Porter's clothes, suits and casual wear, each piece hung and arranged with precision, even down to sleeve length. She walked along the row, her fingers trailing the different textures. She could almost imagine the cloth still carried the heat of the man who wore them.

A half wall sectioned the male and female side of the "closet." Shoes fit into nooks, purses, too. And somehow she knew to push the button on the end—jewelry trays slid out in staggered lengths and heights. The stones that winked at her varied from semiprecious to mind-bogglingly expensive.

Who was she now? In this life? This house with an apartment-sized closet?

Even that thought gave her pause, reminding her that she hadn't grown up with finer things like the ones in this house. How comfortable had she been living here? Had she grown jaded and used to these luxuries?

Glancing back at the elegant driftwood four-poster bed, she began to seriously consider their arrangements as they became reacquainted. He'd said he wouldn't pressure her and she hoped he meant that. He couldn't possibly think they would be sharing a bed. Not yet. In spite of the attraction that still simmered between them, she wasn't ready for intimacy just now.

But someday?

She could barely envision getting through the night, much less through the next few weeks. She turned to the closet again and studied the racks of clothes and rows of shoes and purses and her clothes as if they could give her some hint about the woman she'd been in those missing five years. Certainly one who enjoyed shopping and bright patterns. Grasping at the clothes, she enjoyed the cool feel of the silks and satins. This closet was luxurious—the kind women might fantasize about. Alaina half hoped one of these garments would stir a memory, and the past five years of her life would come rushing back to her.

No such luck.

She released a floor-length gown with a jeweled bodice and glanced down at the simple cotton dress she wore, so different from the rest of her clothes. Had Porter packed this for a reason or had he simply grabbed the first item his hands fell on?

The cotton dress didn't feel like the artsy sense of herself she remembered from five years ago. In fact, the house didn't much reflect her, either. Where was her love of Renaissance art? There were no paintings or statues she would have chosen. Everything was generic, decorator style, matching sets. Had she really spent time here? Been happy?

Where had the traces of herself gone?

The sense of being watched pulled her back into the room, where she found her husband standing by the four-poster bed with a tray of food. He wore a T-shirt and jeans now, the pants low slung on his hips as if he'd lost weight recently. Perhaps he'd been worried sick about her and Thomas. She tried to imagine what the past month had been like for him, but came up empty. It was hard enough for her to grasp her own situation, let alone empathize with his when she didn't know him beyond what the past week had shown her. But all of those interactions had been in the hospital with its sterile environment and lack of privacy. The four and a half years they'd supposedly known each other were wiped clean from her mind. Not so much as a whisper of a memory.

"I thought you might be hungry. There wasn't much of a chance to eat with the trip home, settling Thomas and my mother's surprise arrival." He set the tray on a coffee table in front of the sofa at the foot of their bed. His thick muscled arms flexed, straining against the sleeves of the cotton tee. She tried not to notice, but then felt slightly absurd. He was her husband and yet a stranger all at once.

"That's thoughtful, thank you." She watched him pour the tea, the scent of warm apples and cinnamon wafting upward. "Between a night nanny for the baby and a full-time cook-maid, I'm not sure what I'm going to do to keep myself occupied."

"You've been through a lot. You need your

sleep so you can fully recover. I'm here, too. He's my child."

"Our child."

"Right." Porter's eyes held hers as he passed over the china cup of tea with a cookie tucked on the saucer. "He needs you to be well. We both do."

The warmth of the cup and his words seeped into her and she asked softly, "Where are you planning to sleep?"

He studied her for a slow, sexy blink before responding, "We discussed that in the car."

"Did we?" She wasn't certain about anything right now.

"We did." He sat on the camelback sofa, the four-poster bed big and empty behind him as he cradled a cup of tea for himself in one hand. "But just to be clear, nothing will happen until you're ready. You're recovering on more than one level. I understand that and I respect that. I respect you."

His sensitivity touched her. She should be relieved.

She *was* relieved.

And yet she was also irritated. She couldn't help but notice he still hadn't said he loved her, that he wanted her. He wasn't pushing the physical connection that obviously still hummed between them. Was he giving her space? Was he holding back because she couldn't possibly love a man she didn't know? She kept hoping for some kind of wave of love at first sight. But they were fast approaching more than a few hundred sights and still that wave hadn't hit.

Attraction? Yes. Intrigue? Definitely. But she was also very overwhelmed and still afraid of what those memories might hold. She wasn't able to shake the sense that she couldn't fully trust him. If only he would say the right words to reassure her and calm the nerves in the pit of her belly.

She looked around the room, everything so pristine and new looking, a beach decor of sea-foam greens, tans and white. More of the matched set style that, while tasteful, didn't reflect her preferences in the least. "How often did we come here?"

"I have a work office in the house. So whenever we needed to."

She set aside the tea untouched. "You're so good at avoiding answering my questions with solid information."

A flicker of something—frustration?—flexed his jaw. "We spent holidays here and you spent most of your summers here."

"Then how do I not have any friends in this area?" Where were the casseroles? The welcome home cookies? Or did the überwealthy with maids and night nannies not do that for each other?

"Many people around here are vacationers. Sometimes we invited friends or business acquaintances to stay with us, but they're back home in Tallahassee or at their own holiday vacation houses. We also traveled quite a bit, depending on my work projects."

"So I just followed you around from construction job to job?"

"You make that sound passive. You're anything but that. You worked on your master's degree in art history for two years. One of your professors had connections in the consulting world and our travels enabled you to freelance, assisting museums and private individuals in artwork purchases. You did most from a distance and we flew in for the event proper when artwork arrived."

That was the most he'd said to her at once since she'd woken from her coma. And also very revealing words. "We sound attached at the hip."

He rested his elbows on his knees, staring into his empty teacup. "We were trying to make a baby."

His quiet explanation took the wind right out of her sails. She'd guessed as much since they were adopting and had no other children, but hearing him say it, hearing that hint of pain in his words, made her wonder how much disappointment and grief they'd shared over the years while waiting for their son. Then to have that joy taken from them both because she couldn't remember even the huge landmarks in their relationship that should be ingrained in her mind—when she'd met him, their first kiss, the first time they'd made love…

"And starting our family didn't work the way we planned."

He looked up at her again. "In case you're wondering, the doctors pinpointed it to a number of reasons, part me, part you, neither issue insurmountable on its own, but combined…" He shrugged. "No treatment worked for us, so we decided to adopt."

Thomas. Their child. Her mind filled with the sweet image of his chubby cheeks and dusting of blond hair. "I'm glad we did."

"Me, too," he said with unmistakable love.

The emotion in his voice drew her in as nothing else could have. She sat beside Porter, their shoulders brushing. It was almost comfortable. Or did she want it to be that way? So many emotions tapped at her, dancing in her veins. "He's so beautiful. I hate that I don't remember the first instant I laid eyes on him, the moment I became his mother."

"You cried when the social worker at the hospital placed him in your arms. I'm not ashamed to say I did, too."

Oh, God, this man who'd not once mentioned love could make a serious dent in her heart with only a few words. It was enough to make her want to try harder to fit into this life she didn't remember. To be more patient and let the answers come.

She touched his elbow lightly, wanting the feel of him to be familiar, wanting more than chemistry to connect them. "This isn't the way Christmas was supposed to be for us."

"There was no way to foresee the accident." He placed his hand over hers, the calluses rasping against her skin, another dichotomy in this man who could pay others to do anything for him yet still chose to roll up his sleeves.

"I never did ask how it happened. There have been so many questions I keep realizing I've forgotten to ask the obvious ones."

"We picked up Thomas at the hospital. Since it was so close to our beach house, we considered staying here for the night, but instead opted to drive back home to Tallahassee. A half an hour later, a drunk driver hit us head-on."

"We wanted our son in our own house, in his nursery."

"Something like that."

"What does his nursery look like at our house in Tallahassee?"

"The same as here, countryside with farm animals. You said you wanted Thomas to feel at home wherever he went. Even his travel crib is the same pattern. You even painted the same mural on the wall here."

She remembered admiring the artwork when she'd laid the baby in his crib, enjoying the quiet farm scene with grazing cows and a full blue moon.

"I painted it?" Finally, something of herself in this house of theirs. Her eyes filled with tears. Such a simple thing. A mural for their son in their two homes—or did they have more?—and yet she couldn't remember painting the pastoral scene. She couldn't remember the shared joy over planning for their first child, or the shared tears.

And right now she was seconds away from shedding more tears all over the comfort of Porter's broad chest.

When would she feel she belonged in this life?

Three

Porter woke from a restless sleep. He would have blamed it on staying in the guest room, but he'd bunked here more than once as his marriage frayed. He knew that wasn't the reason he couldn't sleep. Sitting up with the sheets tangled around his waist, he listened closer and heard it again. Someone was awake.

The baby?

He swept the bedding away and tugged on a pair of sweatpants. Even having a night nanny, he couldn't turn off the parenting switch. Over the past few weeks, the accident and time in the hospital had kept him on high alert, fearing the worst 24/7.

A few steps later, he'd padded to the nursery, determined to relieve the night nanny and watch Thomas himself. He'd worked with minimum sleep before. Actually, this past month had made him quite good at operating on only a few hours of rest. He was still so glad his son was okay that being with him was reassuring, even in the middle of the night. Those quiet hours also offered the uninterrupted chance to connect with his child.

Stepping into the doorway, he stopped short. Instead of the matronly granny figure he'd hired to help out, he found his wife feeding their son a bottle in a rocker by the crib.

"Hey, little man," she said softly, propping the bottle on her arm, "I'm your mommy. Forever. And I do want to be your mother. Who wouldn't love that precious face of yours? I wish we could have had the past month together, but that wasn't my choice."

Alaina took his breath away.

Though her pale pink T-shirt was crumpled from sleep, it still hinted at the shape of her curves and the matching pale, striped shorts exposed her beautiful legs.

But Porter couldn't see her face. Like any new mother, she was focused, homed in on her child. Her head was tilted down toward Thomas, blond hair spilling over her right cheek and shoulder.

She was beautiful and the warmth of her love for Thomas pulled at him. For the first time since she had woken up from the coma, she looked at ease. She looked almost happy. If he were being honest with himself, it was the first time she had looked truly happy in months.

A pang of guilt welled in his chest. Porter wanted to do anything—give anything—for her to stay like that. For her to be happy with him again. And she deserved it. Relationships hadn't always been kind to her.

When they'd first started dating four and a half years ago, she had recently left an emotionally abusive boyfriend. He had controlled all aspects of her life, telling her who she could and couldn't see. He'd shown up to check in on her. Slowly isolating her so she would have no one to turn to for help.

That was one of the reasons she didn't have friends around to help now. She'd told him it had been hard to make friends after that experience. Possibly that was why she was struggling so much to trust him now.

He couldn't blame her for feeling that way.

Five years ago, she'd tried to take charge of her life when she'd left the boyfriend. But the abuse hadn't stopped. He'd stalked her. Only the restraining order had given Alaina her life back.

And even after all she'd been through, Porter admired the hell out of that. Her capacity to still love, to still believe in people. It was one of the things that had drawn him to her.

And tonight, he saw that spirit, that beautiful resilient spirit fill the room. A pang of guilt flooded him for not telling her about their marital struggles, but damn it, he couldn't shake the sense he would lose her altogether if he did that. He would do whatever it took to get his family back. He would make sure she had no wants or desires not satisfied.

How had it taken such a terrible accident for him to appreciate how important his family was to him? Shouldn't he have realized all of this on his own, without the fear of almost losing this chance to have a family he of his own?

She must have felt his eyes on her, because she abruptly looked up and met his stare, and the relaxed expression on her face faded. "Porter?"

He quirked an eyebrow. "What good is a night nanny if you don't let her work?"

"I've already missed out on a month of his life. I want him to bond with me."

"You shouldn't push yourself."

"I'm an adult. I know my limits," she said with a tight, bristly tone. Thomas squirmed and whined. She brought him to her shoulder like a natural, patting his back and tapping the rocking chair into motion. "Do you?"

He chuckled drily. "Now that sounds like the wife *I* remember. Yes, I'm a workaholic." He gave her a sideways smile. "But you taught me to slow down and admire art."

"That's a nice thing to say." She patted Thomas's back faster, and still he fussed and squirmed, kicking his casted foot.

"Here, pass him to me." Porter walked deeper into the room, his arms outstretched.

Hurt and irritation flashed in her blue eyes, but she handed over the baby, anyway. "Sure. I want him to be comfortable."

"Alaina," he said, taking the baby and cradling him like a football, while massaging his little leg above the cast, "you aren't expected to know everything any more than I am. We're a team here and together we'll get it all covered."

She nodded once, shoving up from the rocker. "I know. It's just difficult feeling like I bring so little to the table right now."

"You told me once that marriage isn't always fifty-fifty. The pendulum swings back and forth." His mind drifted back to when she'd spoken those words.

She'd been so angry. He'd come home with

a cast on his wrist, fresh out of the emergency room because he'd fallen off a scaffold while inspecting a work site. He'd broken his wrist, but he hadn't wanted to worry her. She'd made it clear she should have been called and included, allowed to help him and drive him home. She'd wanted to tend him and he'd wanted to get to change clothes to go back to work...

He damn well wouldn't let his job interfere with repairing his family now.

Porter felt Thomas drift off to sleep again, his body relaxing. Later he would tell Alaina the baby hadn't been hungry. His leg had been aching from the weight of the cast and the surgery. Alaina felt insecure enough right now. "Let's pass over the nursery monitor to the woman paid to stay awake."

"Sure, but I'm not tired. Maybe it has something to do with that month-long nap I took."

He stifled a laugh to keep from waking the baby, glad that she could joke about their ordeal. He set Thomas in his crib again, stroking the baby's head for a few seconds before turning the monitor back on. Porter nodded to the door and walked into the hall. The night nanny, Mrs. Marks, poked her head out of her bedroom, waved with her puzzle book and ducked into the nursery.

Porter held out a hand to his wife. "Want to see the beach view from the balcony? It was too foggy at supper time to enjoy much. The Christmas lights along the yachts will be more visible now."

"Yachts?"

He winced. From the beginning, she hadn't been comfortable with some parts of their wealthy lifestyle. She'd grown up with hardworking parents who ran a beach food cart in North Carolina's Outer Banks. Their business had paid the bills, but hadn't provided much in the way of extras. What would she say when he told her one of those yachts anchored off the shore was theirs?

"Forget it. You should rest even if you can't sleep."

"I can make decisions for myself," she said with blue fire in her eyes. "Show me the lights."

"Right this way," he said, once again extending his hand to her. Gingerly, she took it, but her grip was loose, as if she was ready to tear away from him at any moment.

Porter led them down the stairs, guided by the muted twinkle of Christmas lights that were twined with garland and wrapped around the banister.

There was an audible silence that followed them, but Porter tried to focus on the fact that she had chosen to come with him instead of retreating to the privacy of her room. It was a good sign.

They reached the stairway landing where the sleek black baby grand piano stood beneath one of Porter's favorite portraits: Alaina in her wedding gown. Her hair had been curled in loose waves that framed her face and the lace wedding gown accentuated her slender figure. She had looked like a princess that day. And it was Porter's renewed intention to make sure he treated her like royalty so she would want to stay once her memory came back. So the good now would overshadow the bad then. That she could forgive and move forward with him and Thomas, building a future.

And if her memory didn't return? He still needed to convince her to stay and build that life with him and their son. Family was everything and he refused to lose his.

Alaina squeezed his hand as they passed in front of the portrait. He watched her gaze lock on the photograph. She didn't say anything for several minutes, and he didn't push her as they strode out onto the patio that overlooked the Atlantic.

Rebuilding his family was a game of growing trust. And she deserved to raise questions without him dumping information on her. He wanted to give her the space she needed to realize she belonged here.

"Tell me about our wedding." The words came out almost like a prayer. Soft. Earnest.

"There's a photo album around the house

somewhere. And plenty of extra pictures on the computer."

"But here's the bridal portrait, and it doesn't tell me anything. Not really. I feel a disconnect with the person in the pictures you've already shown me. Maybe if you tell me, then I will recognize the emotions of the moment."

"Maybe?" His heart hammered.

"Men don't get all emotional about weddings."

He considered her for a moment. She dropped his hand and moved to the piano bench. She sat with her back against the keys, eyes fixed across the room and on the ocean. The Christmas lights from the yachts illuminated the edges of her face, framing her in an otherworldly glow. Damn. She was gorgeous, even when she was stormy. He wanted her in his bed now as much as he ever had. But he wanted to put his family back together even more, and he had to remain focused on the end goal.

Quietly he offered, "I was happy the day we married."

It was true. He had been so entranced by her

sense of the world, by the family they could make together, that he hadn't been able to marry her quickly enough. They'd started trying for children right away. His mother had told him that he and Alaina should take time to cement their relationship. He hadn't given much thought to that—until now.

"How long had we known each other?" Her eyes searched his. He could feel her trying to grasp hold of the past. Of who *they* were.

"We met a year prior. We were engaged for four months of that."

She slid over on the bench and motioned for him to sit next to her. He sat sideways so he could look at her directly.

"Why the rush?"

"We loved each other, knew it was right. Why wait?"

"I wasn't pregnant?"

"No, you weren't. We were never able to conceive."

It had been no one's fault. And they had Thomas now. They had taken in a child who desperately needed a home and stability. And somehow, that seemed to soften the animosity they had felt. They'd agreed to a temporary truce and now he planned to make them a permanent family.

"I hate being dependent on you for all my memories." Her eyes were shining with frustration. But, Porter realized, the frustration wasn't entirely directed at him.

He gently lifted a wisp of hair out of her face and tucked it behind her ear. "Then tell me what your dream wedding day would be like and that will be our wedding memory."

Her eyes went whimsical, a smile pushing dimples into her cheeks. "I would want to get married at a museum, or some historic site on the grounds, but with a preacher there."

Porter nodded to encourage her. "What else?"

"I think I would want a vintage gown and you in an old-school tuxedo, tails perhaps. And if I could dream big—sky's the limit—I would want flowers, so many flowers, all different colors. Southern flowers, magnolias and aza-leas, too."

A long sigh escaped her lips, and she turned in her seat to face him.

"And the reception?"

"A band, so people could enjoy themselves. A buffet meal so people could eat or dance or talk, whatever they wish. I would want there to be children there, activities and a tent where they could play, sitters on hand. How does all of that sound?"

"Very close to the wedding we planned." He took her hand in his and ran his thumb over her silk-smooth palm.

"Planned?"

He shrugged. "My mother put in her two cents, your friends put in theirs. Weddings get com-plicated and we both let them have their way to get things moving so we could start our life to-gether. To be truthful, I just remember you and how beautiful you looked and how damn lucky I was to have convinced you to marry me."

More memories hit him, about how later she'd

come to resent not having stood her ground to have the wedding of her dreams. Her insistence that her style and wishes got pushed aside by his mother and wedding planners.

She inched toward him on the bench, resting a hand on his knee. Her touch made his blood surge hot beneath his skin. Damn. He wanted to take her in his arms. Wanted to taste her kiss. To taste *her*—over and over until they both stopped thinking and remembering.

"That's lovely, what you just said and the way you described the feelings. I wish I recalled even a part of that." The murmur leaped from her lips as her eyes searched his face. There was intrigue there, sure. Attraction, definitely.

"You will. Someday."

Another deep sigh. "And if I don't?"

"Then we'll keep taking things a day at a time and looking to the future. Marriage isn't perfect, Alaina. You've forgotten the arguments and disagreements, too. So perhaps it's a trade-off, getting to start over with a clean slate."

Alaina shook her head, but didn't pull away.

Her fingers continued to trace light circles on his knee. "Amnesia is a horrible illness, not some trade-off. I would gratefully welcome one bad memory now from those years, just to open the door. To see our life together."

"What if that one memory made you stop loving me because you couldn't recall the rest?"

He wanted this fresh start for their family so badly. He needed it down to his core. And he was afraid that if she recalled any of the past year, she'd pack up and be out of his life the way she'd intended to do before the accident.

"I don't mean to be harsh, but I can't remember falling in love with you. So how is that a point?"

He threw her a playful wink. "I guess I'll just have to help you fall in love with me again."

She didn't smile back, her gaze narrowing with intensity. "So do you still love me?"

"Of course I do," he said automatically because that's what she needed to hear.

But from the look in her eyes, he could tell

that on some level, behind the amnesia, she sensed the truth.

This wasn't about loving or not loving each other. After all, they hadn't spoken those words to each other in over a year. This second chance was about finally building the family he'd always wanted and doing whatever it took to make that happen.

Alaina leaned against the door frame of Porter's home office, making the most of the moment to study him unobserved. Much like as he'd watched her last night in the nursery. She'd been more moved by the way he'd looked at her, almost as if he was thinking the words he never spoke. Words about loving her.

Why was it so important to hear that from him when she didn't know how she felt about him? When she couldn't remember meeting him, marrying him—falling for him? And some men weren't overly demonstrative.

What about him?

She searched for clues as she watched him

work at his computer, seated behind an over-size desk. He wore casual clothes, jeans and a polo shirt, his watch the only cue to his wealth. She liked that about him, how if she'd met him on the street she wouldn't have guessed he had all these houses—and a closet as big as some apartments.

She also liked the artwork on the wall behind him. Nice choice. It fit him more than a lot of things in this elaborate vacation place. She wondered if she'd picked it out for him.

He wore thick black-framed glasses as he typed, something she hadn't noticed before. There was so much about him she didn't know. So much to learn and on the one hand, some would say she had all the time in the world. But she felt an urgency to settle her life, for Thomas's sake.

And she couldn't ignore how much it touched her heart to see her son snoozing in a bassinet beside Porter's leather office chair. That he'd made arrangements to watch the baby while working spoke volumes. She could see that Porter wanted to be a good father, that he wanted to be active in his son's upbringing. She wanted to trust her impressions of him and accept that she had an amazing life. She wanted to quit worrying about the past she couldn't remember.

And yet she couldn't dismiss the sense that she should be wary of assuming everything was as it seemed.

Porter glanced up, as if sensing her gaze. He tucked his reading glasses on top of his head, his eyes were full of awareness from their almost kiss earlier.

Even if she couldn't remember what they'd had, she could swear she felt all those shared kisses in their past on some level. Did he have regrets about them as a couple? Was that the unsettled feeling she sensed in him?

Had he appreciated what they had?

"Alaina," he said softly, rocking back in his chair. "I've got this. Easy. He's sleeping. Go relax. Take a walk on the beach. Read a book."

Or stay with Porter and be tempted even more? How long would she be able to resist?

Not long.

She backed out of the door. "Sure, thanks. I'll have my cell phone with me. Don't hesitate to call if you need me to come back for him. I want to be with him whenever he's awake."

She'd missed so much already. Oh, God, she was going to start crying if she kept thinking about it.

Her emotions were swinging from desire for her stranger of a husband to grief over all she'd lost. She needed to get herself under control or she would be a nervous wreck. Thomas didn't need to have all those negative feelings around him. Maybe Porter was right about her taking time to decompress for a while.

With determined strides she moved toward the kitchen, scarfed down some toast and tea, and contemplated the events of her past twenty-four hours.

A whirlwind didn't even begin to cover it.

Glancing around the open space, she couldn't help but feel the decor looked as if it had been directly lifted from a catalog. Everything was gorgeous—stainless steel appliances with rustic wooden accent bowls—but it all felt too… put together.

Was this the kind of woman she had become over the past five years?

Unable to suppress her need for more answers, Alaina began to explore the house. Their house, she reminded herself. This was supposedly all hers, too, even if it felt alien in comparison to her more Spartan upbringing. She needed to learn to be comfortable here again.

Porter had made it clear that he wanted her to relax. To take time for herself. And while that was sweet, she wasn't entirely sure she enjoyed being forced into downtime. She had lost so much of her life that downtime intimidated her.

But she had to admit she admired Porter's dedication to Thomas. It was endearing. He had found a way to integrate work and family. And that trait was sexy as hell.

She searched for more signs of encouragement regarding their life, but the rest of the house mirrored the kitchen. It was also well put together. So manicured and manufactured. She couldn't seem to find a trace of her artistic side at all.

Alaina thought back to the last apartment she could remember, the one she'd had five years ago. It had been modest, but hanging above her bed, she had placed a Renaissance-style painting. The myths drew her in. She loved that each painting captured a Greek tragedy or legend.

There wasn't one painting like that in this whole place.

Did Porter hate that sort of thing? Had she given up her taste in favor of his? And should she just start changing things now?

The bramble of her thoughts was interrupted as she came to the staircase and practically walked into her mother-in-law.

Courtney's hair was swept into a tight but elegant topknot. Polished. Her green dress swished as she moved toward Alaina. Jimmy Choo heels clicked with each step.

The poised, older woman waved with long, manicured nails. "Come with me. I need coffee.

Or a mimosa. Unless you would rather some time by yourself?"

"Of course not." Alaina had too much time to spend with a jumble of questions about her missing thoughts. "I would love the chance to visit with you."

Her mother-in-law cast her a sidelong glance. "Dear, it's all right. You don't have to tiptoe around my feelings."

"I welcome the chance to get to know you. You're Porter's mom." She extended her arm for Courtney to take. It was time to start to get to know her family. Her old life.

Had they got along before?

Courtney linked her arm with Alaina's. "I'm also your mother-in-law. Thomas's grandmother. I'm here to help however I can. Not that you really need it. You're very good with Thomas."

Was she? God, she hoped so. "I don't know anything about babies."

"Maybe not before you got married, but since I've known you? You've learned a lot about infants. You volunteered in the NICU three times a week, holding the newborns or just talking to the ones too tiny and fragile to be held." Her mother-in-law guided her back toward the kitchen.

Back toward Porter.

"I did that?" Another thing to add to the list of things she was learning about her life during these missing years. Fancy art exhibits. A postgraduate degree. NICU babies. She had certainly filled her time while married to Porter.

"It was hard for you, wanting to be a mother so desperately." Courtney patted her hand. Sympathy radiated from her touch.

There was a certain calm that settled between them. An understanding Alaina seemed to be close to grasping, but couldn't quite settle. Not yet. Although it wouldn't hurt to ask a few questions.

"What about Porter? Does he want to be a father?"

"Of course he does. You've seen how he is with Thomas."

Alaina thought back to the way he had massaged Thomas's hurt leg last night. About how he had insisted on watching him as he worked. He was taking his fatherly duties seriously. And it made her heart melt.

"Whose idea was it to adopt?"

Her mother-in-law hesitated midstep before walking again, heels clicking on travertine tiles. "You would have to ask him that question."

Did Courtney not know or was there something deeper here? An argument within the family? "I'm so tired of asking him about every single detail of our lives together. I was hoping you could help fill in some details."

"I'm sorry about the amnesia, dear." She squeezed Alaina's hand, her touch lotiony soft. "That has to be so frustrating, but maybe you can focus on the good things, like your child, your marriage, your home. Not everyone has all of that."

The woman was such a mix of coolness and warmth. One minute Alaina was certain her mother-in-law disapproved of her, and the next Courtney was offering genuine comfort. Navigating life lately was like walking through a maze with a blindfold on.

"I hear what you're saying and I appreciate your trying to help. Really." They were practically at Porter's office now. Alaina glanced at the wall that housed photographs in handsome frames. Not one photograph had Alaina side by side with Courtney.

Glancing at her mother-in-law, Alaina chewed on her lip. What had their relationship been like? Judging by the photo albums she'd pored over, there wasn't much of a relationship between them. She forced herself to ask the question that had weighed on her mind since Porter announced that Courtney was at their vacation house. "Did you and I like each other?"

Arched eyebrows lifted. "Honestly? Not very much. We don't have a lot in common."

Finally, what felt like an honest answer from someone. "I think I like you now."

"That's probably because you don't feel married to my son."

True as it was, the declaration stung. Alaina spun her wedding ring around on her finger.

"And could it also be that you don't see me as Porter's wife anymore?"

"Maybe…" Courtney paused, worrying one fingernail with another. "I made my mistakes—you made yours. But lucky for us, we get a fresh start."

There was a lot of fresh-starting going around. A lot of work going into creating a second chance at her life. If only she knew how long it would be until her memories came back. If they ever would. Was the effort to start over wasted—or vitally necessary?

Either way, right now, Alaina had no choice but to press on. "Courtney, will I dislike you again if I remember? Was it that bad?"

And if she remembered, what would she think of her marriage? That was a question she couldn't bring herself to ask.

"Somehow, I think we've found a middle ground that will stick regardless of what you remember."

"Good. I need a friend I can trust." And she meant it. Whatever had been in the past between them—well, it didn't matter right now.

Alaina wasn't that person anymore. While it hadn't been long ago since she'd woken up in that hospital, the accident and the amnesia had changed her irrevocably. "So? Can we be friends?"

"Friends. I like that. No mother-daughter mess. I'm not your mother. Hell, I'm having enough trouble getting used to being a grandmother. And just so we're clear, I don't change diapers. But I excel at watching while a baby naps and I'm superb at holiday shopping." Courtney winked a perfect smoky eye.

"I'm not going to be ready for that anytime soon." The idea of going out in public was absolutely overwhelming. And venturing out in public at Christmastime? That sounded dreadful.

Claustrophobic.

"That's why we're going to shop online. Later, of course, once you've had time to settle in and recover." Courtney stopped outside her son's office door and tapped lightly until Porter glanced up. "Since the baby is napping, that's my call to be a grandmother. Son, take your wife out and romance the socks off her."

Four

His mom walked away from the office door, heels click-clacking in time with her singsong voice as she spoke to Thomas. He hadn't expected his mom to embrace the grandmother gig so wholeheartedly, but then his life was anything but predictable these days.

Porter searched Alaina's expression. The tension in her jaw. The way her brow furrowed as she subconsciously drew one arm across her midsection to grasp the opposite upper arm.

She gave him a good-natured grin, but it was clear she was still unsure of how to act around him. He couldn't blame her for that.

But she also looked ready to bolt and that's the last thing he wanted, so he took the time to take her in. Alive. Vibrant. Here, with him and Thomas. Thank God.

On top of her head, she'd piled her hair in a loose, messy bun. Wavy blond strands fell out of the bun, framing her slender face.

Her white dress hugged her breasts, drawing his eyes. Tempting him. Reminding him of the heat they'd always found in bed. The passion that still simmered between them, that they could find again if he could make the most of this time. His hands ached to stroke the fabric along her skin, to caress her along the length of the dress that fell in rolling pleats from her waist, to trace the red flower embroidery snaking around at midthigh.

To press his mouth behind her knee and tunnel his way up her skirt.

She looked like a vision right out of *The Nutcracker*. Clara, as she ran away with the Nutcracker Prince. The only question was, could he be that prince again? Could he charm her, show her how damn great they were together? Somewhere along the years the fantasy had given way to a reality that neither of them had anticipated.

And he hated that.

And he hated that the reality had broken their family, nearly ending the life he'd dreamed of as a boy.

Though she lacked memories, every item she'd added to the house screamed its sentimentality. It was like alarms blaring. The dress she wore was no different.

It was the same dress she had worn two years ago, on their vacation to St. Augustine. They were only supposed to be in town for the night. He had surprised her after a major art opening by booking a charming bed-and-breakfast room for the weekend. They'd spent the whole time laughing, drinking local wine. Back when things were simpler. When they still sparkled and sizzled together.

It could be that way again.

It would be that way again. He refused to accept any other outcome.

"Don't let my mother get to you or put pressure on you when it comes to our marriage."

It was the best he had to offer. Wooing her back into this family was a delicate task requiring finesse.

"There's not much you could do to romance a new mom who's recovering from amnesia." She tapped her forehead in jest.

"That sounds like a challenge." He thrived on a challenge.

"Okay—" she spread her arms wide "—give it your best shot."

"Really? You want me to sweep you off your feet?" He cocked his head to the side, a thrill zipping through him.

"Sure, what woman wouldn't want to be swept off her feet?" Inclining her head, she dramatically twirled. The fabric of her skirt tightened and loosed as she turned. She was so damn sexy.

And he wanted her for his own.

"Challenge accepted." Progress. He could practically taste it.

She stopped midspin. "Wait, never mind. This shouldn't be a game."

"Believe me—I understand that all too well." Closing the gap between them, he rested his hands on her shoulders. "So relax. I've got this under control. Let me pamper you, and you focus on recuperating."

"You're right. The best thing I can do for my family is to regain my memory so we can move forward with our future rather than staying here in limbo with you working from home at a vacation house." She twisted her hands nervously, glancing out the window. "Honestly, I believe it's too soon for us to go on some extravagant outing."

So large gestures were out of the question. It was time for a game plan. He knew he had to be quick. They couldn't hole up in this house forever. Her memory would slowly come back into focus. It was time for action. Now.

Still, he said, "Of course. I agree and I have a few ideas, but I'll need a half hour to pull things together. There's a hammock past the pool, by the shore. I'll meet you there."

Her smile was hopeful. Beautiful. "Sounds perfect."

Alaina inhaled deep breaths of ocean air, one after the other, a foot draped over the side of the hammock, toe tapping to keep the steady swaying motion. The hammock was attached to two fat palm trees, branches and fronds rustling overhead.

Could Porter really find a way to put her fears to rest? Could regaining her memory be as simple as relaxing and enjoying time with the man she'd married?

She wanted to believe that. It had only been a week since she'd woken up after all. Yet, every hour that passed with no breakthroughs knotted the anxiety tighter within her.

Answers. That was what she needed. She was desperate for them. She kept hoping the scenery would jog her memory. Bestow the memories that were locked away somewhere in her mind.

Glancing at the harbor, she tried to imagine what sort of person she had grown into. A twenty-eight-year-old woman with a husband rich enough to bump elbows with the incredibly wealthy. And, judging by the sheer size of the yachts before her, incredibly wealthy didn't even begin to cover it.

Yachts spotted the water with the same frequency as white caps in a storm. A few of them looked like personal cruise ships.

Had she been out on any of these? Did she move comfortably in a world like this? Knowing what her life had been like before, she couldn't imagine it.

Her thoughts were cut short as a sun-bronzed woman approached. Alaina guessed the woman was probably a decade older than her. Maybe more. But older, Alaina realized, was a matter of perspective. She still felt as if she was looking through the eyes of a twenty-three-year-old.

The woman bustled toward Alaina, brunette hair flapping beneath an oversize white floppy hat. Cat-eyed sunglasses shielded the majority of her face, concealing her eyes from view. The gust of wind tugged at her bright pink-and-peach shift dress.

Alaina stood with mixed feelings. On the one hand, she was glad to have someone else to talk to, but on the other, she was nervous. It was too soon. What if the woman asked something Alaina couldn't answer?

But then hadn't she just thought how she needed to push ahead? She had to be strong, brave, for Thomas.

And Porter.

The woman jogged the last few steps and hugged Alaina hard before stepping back, her hands clasped to her chest. "Oh my God, Alaina, I thought that was you." The woman scrunched her nose, crinkling zinc oxide into the creases. "I forgot for a minute you can't remember all of us. I'm Sage Harding. Your neighbor. I like to think I'm your friend, even if we only see each other a couple of times a year for holidays."

A couple of times a year? But Porter had said they came here often. Perhaps Sage didn't come as often and so their paths only crossed a couple of times a year. Alaina wanted to believe that. Porter had no reason to lie.

She didn't understand her need to believe the worst in him, to be so suspicious of his every word.

They were married. There was ample proof. And they'd adopted a child together. They had a beautiful life—if she could just bring herself to accept it.

"Thank you for coming over to speak to me, Sage. That makes me feel less like an amnesia freak or a patient."

"Honey, you can't help what happened to you." Sage sat on a teal Adirondack chair next to the hammock. "You were in a car accident."

"I understand the facts in my mind, but it's difficult to trust my mind these days." She rolled her eyes at her own lame joke. "But enough about my medical woes. Tell me about yourself. Where are you from? Are you here with your family? How did we become friends?"

"Wow, that's a lot of questions." Sage held

up her fingers, holiday-green glitter polish on short nails. "I'm from the D.C. area. My husband's in the House of Representatives, so we keep this house to stay Florida residents. Our two kids go to boarding school. And you and I became friends at an art gallery fund-raiser for the homeless."

That all rang true and fit with everything Porter had been telling her. "What type of art do you enjoy?"

"Oh, I don't know jack about art." Sage waved a self-deprecating hand. "I was there for the canapés, champagne and movie-star company. And helping the homeless. I like being a part of charity work. It's a rewarding way to spend my time."

"That's nice." Alaina wasn't sure what else to say to this refreshingly honest woman.

Sage leaned closer, her elbows on her knees. "Are you okay, really okay? I've been so worried. I came by the hospital when I heard and left flowers. But you weren't allowed to have visitors. I would have a baby shower for you, but that might be awkward just now. Maybe we'll wait until you get your memory back."

"I think that's best. And I'm still…resting."

"Oh, right. Silly me. I didn't mean to intrude. I was just so glad to see you and wanted to make sure you and Porter are doing okay."

Now that was a loaded statement. Alaina opted for an answer that wouldn't land her in hot water. "We're enjoying being parents."

"How is your little guy's foot?"

"Healing."

"I'm so relieved." Sage studied her matching Christmas-green toenails for three crashes of the waves. "I wasn't sure you would be back this year after, well, your male visitor last Christmas."

Alaina forced herself to stay still. There was no answer to that revelation and she sure as hell wasn't going to quiz a virtual stranger. "Thank you for stopping by."

"I shouldn't have said anything. I thought maybe he'd contacted you and I wanted to be sure you knew. I mean well." She pushed to her feet and dusted sand off her legs. "Please accept my apology."

"Accepted. It's tough to know the right thing to say. Amnesia isn't an everyday occurrence and it's difficult to know how to handle it." Alaina stood and saw Porter walking down the bluff carrying a picnic basket and an insulated bag. "There's my husband."

Sage crinkled her nose again. "That's my cue to leave."

"Merry Christmas to you and your family."

"To you and yours, too, honey." Sage squeezed Alaina's hand quickly. "Enjoy your baby's first visit from Santa Claus."

Santa Claus?

Of course. She should be focusing on Thomas's first Christmas. On doing normal family things like picking out toys for him to enjoy over the next year. Or making Christmas cookies, as her mother had always done as far back as Alaina could remember. Starting her own family traditions with Porter.

Or had they had traditions? Tough to tell in

this generic-looking house without her own personal stamp.

She wanted that homey holiday life so desperately. Wanted to be normal again. To be herself again. Whatever that meant and whoever that was.

If things were normal, she and Porter might be standing in line somewhere, debating how to spoil their beautiful new son.

Anxiety ebbed back into her chest. Not that it was ever far away.

The thought of melting away into a crowd sounded a lot more appealing now than it had earlier.

A quick glance back down the sandy path toward the vacation home revealed that Porter had already started to make his way toward her. He was only about ten feet away and just the sight of him took her breath away all over again.

She allowed herself to examine him fully as he approached, basket in hand. His broad shoulders and chest, the clear suggestion of muscles beneath his casual light blue button-down. The way his jawline appeared to be chiseled out of marble. Strong. Defined. Like some of the statues she used to have in her old apartment.

But it was the lightness in his demeanor, the force of his smile that made her heart hammer. While he was made up of hard angles, his smile made him seem approachable. Understanding. Maybe even affectionate.

Was that what she'd seen in him from the first?

She wanted to kiss him. To know what they were like together. In bed. Or in the shower. Or in the dozens of other places her imagination wandered with fantasies.

Or were those memories? She couldn't be sure. There had been an undeniable physical connection between them from the moment she'd seen him in the hospital. It had laced each of their conversations so far. Amnesia or not, that much of a connection had persisted.

How could she have looked at another man as Sage had not too subtly insinuated?

Alaina had wondered more than once if Porter had been hiding something from her. She just hadn't considered that whatever he might be hiding was her fault.

Sunglasses shielding his eyes from the late-morning sun, Porter jogged down the last step cut into the bluff, his deck shoes hitting sand. He'd expected to find his wife napping in the hammock. Not chatting with their gossipy neighbor. Hell, he'd even checked with the staff to make sure the Hardings wouldn't be here for Christmas.

Apparently, staff intel was wrong.

Sage Harding fanned a wave at him as she slid her own sunglasses back on her face and sashayed through the sea oats and around a bluff back to her white mansion on stilts.

Between his mother and Sage, he couldn't catch a break. Although a voice in the back of his mind persisted that he didn't deserve one. He was deliberately keeping parts of their past from his wife. He tamped down that voice, not just for his own reasons but for her sake, as well.

The doctor had said not to push her, but rather to let her recover the missing years on her own.

All the CT scans and MRI scans hadn't shown any brain damage, and yet her coma had persisted. The doc had said her mind was most likely protecting herself from something she wasn't ready to deal with. Again that voice piped up that maybe she didn't want to recall how close they'd been to signing the divorce papers their lawyers had drawn up. That she wanted this second chance at creating a family every bit as much as he did.

His pace quickened as he approached. He could see that there was something sparking beneath the surface of her eyes. It was in the way she cocked her head to the side and studied him up and down. A question in her expression. A curiosity. One he wanted to answer.

Time was limited now as their son napped— and the holidays were a brief interlude, too. Soon, they would have to return home. She would find out all that he'd been keeping from her and all hell could break loose. He intended to use this time with her, away from all that, wisely.

Porter placed the picnic basket and insulated bag on the Adirondack chair so there would be nowhere to sit except beside his wife. "You'll want to stay clear of Sage Harding."

"Sage?" Alaina shifted, the roped hammock swaying beneath her. "Why on earth should I avoid her?"

"Because she's not as genuine as she tries to appear. She's cultivating wealthy friends to fund her husband's run for the US Senate. Plain and simple, she uses people."

Alaina slowly nodded as if she was unsure how to respond. As if she didn't trust his word. Ouch.

"Okay. That's sad to hear, that someone's using others."

"You're not sure if you believe me about Sage's motivations for coming over?"

She shook her head. "It's not that. But people can have different impressions of someone."

A diplomatic answer. But one that reminded

him he still had to earn her trust. Well, re-earn. "Fair enough. It's your judgment call to make. Just promise me you'll be careful around her."

"I will." She chewed her bottom lip. "Maybe I was too eager to believe what she said about being friends because I feel so isolated. There's no one I know outside of our family."

"You asked for phone numbers. I looked up ones for your old friends." He held out a sheet of paper with scribbled names and numbers. It was a small gesture, but he hoped it would matter to her. Show her that he was committed to making their family work.

"*Old* friends? We're not friends anymore?"

"You moved away from North Carolina years ago. They got married, too, and many of them relocated, as well." He shrugged. "People lose touch with each other. It happens."

She pressed her forehead. "Not that it really matters anyway, I guess. They would only know what I already recall. They won't have much of anything to offer about the past five years other than maybe one of those 'the world is rosy' Christmas letters I must have sent out." The hurt and frustration in her voice filled each syllable.

"Maybe there's something they can offer. I want you to be happy. I'm trying to help you, Alaina."

"And I'm not trying?" she snapped. "This is so very hard, not remembering even meeting you, yet trying to be a wife and a mother in a completely alien world."

This wasn't going the way he'd planned. He didn't want her to feel more isolated, more alone. "I'm sorry. I know this is a million times tougher on you, and I want to help you." He smoothed back her hair, his hand resting lightly on her shoulder. "I didn't mean to upset you. Can we start over? I've ordered brunch. You barely touched breakfast. Okay?"

"Sure, Porter, that's probably a good idea. I'm sorry for lashing out at you like that. I know this has to be difficult for you, too. And I can see you're truly trying to make things easier for me." She pressed her fingers to her temple again as if her head was throbbing. "Did we used to argue like that a lot?"

Arguments?

He needed to tread warily as hell on this topic.

It was such a loaded question she'd asked. And a difficult one to answer.

Porter reached into the basket to give himself time to think, and hefted out an impressive spread. Brie. Herbed crackers. Fresh fruit, cut and quartered. Dark chocolate–covered nuts. All of her absolute favorites. Years ago, when things were easier between them, they had made brunches on the beach a ritual. It was also how they had spent their first date. A picnic on the beach.

"We exchanged words, and yes, we argued." He glanced back at her, looking over the top of his sunglasses. "Our reconciliations were incredible." He handed her a piece of chocolate.

She eyed him pensively for a few seconds before her shoulders relaxed and she took the truffle with a playful smile, blue eyes twinkling like the ocean reflecting the sun. "It's not sexy to hit on a woman who just came out of a coma."

"Why?" He pivoted on one knee, cupping the side of her face in one hand. "You're beautiful."

She didn't pull away. "I'm pasty and exhausted."

"That's why this is the perfect place to rest." He pulled a slice of cheese from the cutting board and popped it into her mouth before she could respond. "Now eat. You need to put back on the weight you lost."

Her throat moved in a swallow before she said, "Was that an insult?"

"I just told you. You've always been beautiful to me." He traced her bottom lip with his thumb. "I'm more than willing to practice our reconciliation skills whenever you're ready."

She nipped the pad of his thumb and sent a jolt of arousal clean through him.

"Porter, I would be lying if I said I wasn't tempted. So much." She pressed a kiss into his work-roughened palm before moving his hand away. "But you're right about me lacking energy and needing to refuel. And you were right about me needing to decompress. My emotions seem to swing from high to low without warning."

"Damned by my own words," he said, but glad for the reminder to put her needs first.

"And we should go back soon. The baby..."

"Is sleeping. With my mother watching and a nanny as backup." He frowned, shaking his head. "Because I would never trust my mother as the sole caregiver of a child. Our child."

"That's sad."

"I meant it as a joke." Sorta.

"Really? Because I don't think it's funny. Is that why you have the nanny? Because you don't trust me?"

He could hear her winding up again.

"I trust you with our child, unequivocally. Truly, I only want you to rest." They needed the extra help right now until things returned to a normal routine. Because it had to return to normal. He refused to accept the possibility he could lose the family they had created for their son.

"You're maxed out, as well."

He rubbed the back of his neck and didn't answer.

Didn't quite look at her.

She ran her hand slowly along his shoulders. Her fingers lightly tracing circles down his back, reigniting his desire. She inched closer, so her head was inches from his. Her voice lowered, filling with concern. With understanding.

"And having your mother here stresses you more."

He reached out, closing the distance between them. Hand to her cheek, he stroked her skin with his thumb. She sighed into his hand, her breath warm against him. Sexy and moist. He wanted her so damn much.

"Damn it, Alaina, you always did read me well, right from the start."

Unable to resist a taste, just this one moment to connect with his wife again, Porter leaned in to kiss her.

Five

The warmth of his lips sent an electric pulse through her, and she hungered for more. His hand wound into her hair. Alaina's own body melted into his as she pressed herself against his hard, muscled chest.

The kiss deepened, mouths opening, hands stroking. Alaina's desire became more urgent as she tasted a hint of raspberries on his tongue. He angled her closer, tongue exploring. Testing. Her fingers curled into the fine texture of his shirt. Everything about him drew her, from the way he looked at her to the way he made her smile. From the way he touched her to the care he gave their child.

Right now, she could easily envision how she'd fallen in love with this man and married him. She ached to remember the passionate experiences they'd shared, words they'd exchanged. Anything. And she hated that he had it all and she had nothing.

But she reveled in how hard he was working to win her over. That thrilled her and excited her—

From somewhere outside of this wonderful moment, she heard the distinctive hum of a speedboat skidding across the water. It snapped her to her senses. Reminded her of the fact she was kissing a man she didn't really know, a man she didn't fully trust, which complicated her feelings even more.

She pushed against his chest. Broke the kiss and connection before looking shyly at him.

She laughed self-consciously. "I shouldn't have done that. You have an amnesiac wife and a new baby and here I am making a move on you."

He burst out laughing, the sound rolling out on the ocean breeze. He laughed again, his head falling and broad shoulders shaking. Pinching the bridge of his nose, he said, "God, woman, you turn me inside out. You always have."

The words sent a shiver through her every bit as arousing as his kiss had been. There was emotion behind the words.

Had there been emotion in his touch, as well? She didn't trust her judgment yet.

The wind blew her hair across her face and she swept it away again. "I'm sorry. I, um, didn't mean to send mixed signals and mislead you—"

He traced her lips. "You turning me inside out has always been a good thing. We may have argued about a lot of issues, but we always connected on a physical level." He tapped her lips a final time. "But I meant it when I said I wouldn't pressure you to take this faster than you want to take it."

"That's good to know." She shot to her feet

restlessly, gathering up their lunch and putting it back in the basket. "The attraction between us is…problematic."

An urgency to move filled her. They needed to get back to the baby, anyway. She gathered more remnants of the picnic, sliding the lids onto the various containers. But not before she snagged another piece of brie and popped it into her mouth. She reveled in the creamy texture, using the food-induced silence to steady herself.

"We were married for years," he said into the silence. "Even if your brain doesn't remember, I believe that on some level your body does. We'll take things slowly until your mind catches up." He offered her another piece of dark chocolate. Her fingertips gingerly brushed his as she took it. Another confusing jolt of desire burst through her.

"What if my mind doesn't ever catch up?"

A devilish smile spread across his lips. "Then we'll start over."

"And what if I'm not the same woman I was?"

In her chest, her heart pounded. Tension rose again, unmistakable.

"You are the woman I met five years ago."

She left the hammock, placing the basket on the chair and stacking the containers inside. "But I'm not. I recall what I was like then. It feels like it just happened. But the past week, waking up and finding out that I'm married and a mother and I have this whole chunk of life I lived? That was a surprise. That's changed me. Immeasurably."

"Sure, of course it did."

"You say that. But I don't think you're hearing me. Not really. You seem to want to pick up where we left off."

On a certain level, she could understand that desire. On the logical level. But the emotional one—that was an entirely different scenario. How could she make him understand how overwhelming all of this was?

His jaw flexed and he left the hammock, helping her pack their meal, kneeling beside her.

"I'm trying to help you remember, like you asked."

"I don't believe that. You want me to be the woman you married. To have our lives back the way they were."

He snorted on a dark laugh. "You couldn't be further from the truth."

She went still, sagging back to sit on her butt in the sand. A chill settled in her stomach. "So things weren't great between us."

"I didn't say that."

"When I asked you if we argued a lot, you answered that we exchanged words and had great make-up sex."

"We did."

"But we argued. A lot." She packed up the last few items into the basket. And shut it hard.

"Married couples do that."

"We did."

"Yes, Alaina, we did." He clasped her shoulders. "We weren't perfect. We still aren't. But we have a chance here to build our family.

We've been wanting this for a long time. Can you believe that much at least?"

He searched her face, scrutinized her expression. Cheeks ablaze, she tried to work out the harrowing emotions that knocked against each other inside of her like kids in bumper cars. He was asking for her trust. And she *should* trust him. They were married after all—but she had been close to having an affair, if Sage Harding was to be believed. What did all of that add up to?

Porter was practically a stranger to her. And his desire to have her put her faith in him frayed her nerves more. It didn't make sense. The Porter she was meeting now had never given her a reason not to trust him. But deep down, something stopped her from giving herself over to him completely.

"Sure," she said, knowing her answer was a brush-off and not able to come up with more than, "I believe you want to build a family."

Dizziness hit. Her chest tightened. She felt a moment of panic over being confined even though he was just holding her. She knew the fear was unreasonable, but still, given what had happened in that past abusive relationship. she couldn't help but feel nervous over how isolated she'd allowed herself to become. And how some might say Porter had taken away her resources by bringing her here where she wasn't close to anyone, just as her old boyfriend had done before.

What did she really know about this man beyond that he was gentle with Thomas?

Her arms began to tingle. Alaina felt so boxed in by the weight of the past she remembered and the past she didn't. Space. That's what she needed. She shot up from their beach picnic, turned on her heel…

And ran.

The pounding of her feet hitting the ground reverberated in her mind. She hadn't even noticed she had balled her hands into fists until she made it to the kitchen. The sticky sweet remains of a raspberry fell into the sink as she unclenched her fingers.

One deep breath. And then another.

There was no one to call. It was times like these that she desperately wished she could talk to her mother or father. They had always known what to say, how to help her parse out a situation. But they had died during her junior year of college. The memory of that moment, of that horrible phone call, was still fresh in her mind.

She'd give anything for her family to be intact.

Didn't Thomas deserve the same? An intact, functional family? Parents who adored him? She already loved her son so much. And if she were being honest with herself, she wanted a family just as much as Porter seemed to. She wanted them to be a complete and intact unit.

More than her own happiness was at stake now.

And for the first time, she was more afraid of what might happen to her marriage if she remembered, than if she left those five years buried.

* * *

Relieved Thomas's checkup had gone so well, Porter shut the door of the car behind his wife in the parking lot of the pediatrician's office. This had been their first joint trip off the property since the family had left the hospital together last week. He glanced in the backseat, where Thomas smiled at him in his "Santa's Little Helper" onesie.

The doctor had confirmed that Thomas was healing well. It would just take time. That seemed to be the theme of his life recently. Wait. Be patient.

It was damn hard to do sometimes. Porter strode around the car and positioned himself in the driver's seat. On the one hand, he was grateful they were all still together. On the other hand, he felt as if things had stalled since their beach picnic. She had built a wall around herself and he didn't understand why. Since that kiss, she'd been antsy, jumpy over being touched. Only when they were with Thomas were they both at ease. He didn't doubt for an instant—she loved their son every bit as much as he did. That baby boy had them wrapped around his finger.

Porter had built multimillion-dollar homes around the country. He'd built a billion-dollar corporation on his own, with no help from his wealthy mother. And yet those accomplishments didn't mean as much to him as coaxing a big belch from Thomas or laughing with Alaina as they struggled to work a tiny flying fist into a sleeper.

He wanted a family no matter what. People accused him of being determined at work, but that was nothing compared to how hard he would devote himself to making this come together. He wouldn't give up what he was building in his life. It was a helluva lot more important than any structure put up by his corporation.

Porter started the car and adjusted the radio. "Would you like to pick up carryout on our way home or stop by a deli? The weather's perfect to eat on the deck."

Would she be interested in unwinding later in the hot tub? He didn't know what to expect from her after she'd welcomed his kiss on the beach, and then proceeded to push him away.

"Porter, do you mind if we do something away from the beach house? I don't want to be cooped up all day. It's too nice of an afternoon to spend inside." Alaina stared out the window as they drove past a team of reindeer made of bent willow branches in the courtyard of the doctor's office.

A smile pulled at his lips. Perhaps this patience thing was paying off. Alaina hadn't wanted to do anything outside of the house since they'd arrived there. This was a good sign. Maybe she was beginning to trust him.

"Of course. I have to swing by a job site for a final walk-through. Then the rest of the day is ours." He reached for her hand and gave it a gentle squeeze.

"I don't mind that at all. Besides, I'd like to see you in action."

She flashed him a quick smile as she turned the radio to a Christmas station. Her head bopped along to a jazzy rendition of an old classic as they drove through town, where lighted white snowflakes hung from palm trees lining the village's main thoroughfare.

It didn't take long to reach the job site. This was an up-and-coming section of town. The beach stretched and wound lazily in front of them, beyond the Spanish-influenced mansion Porter needed to inspect.

"Porter, this place is beautiful. It's so exotic looking." Her eyes darted to the lattice that was pressed against the side of the house between the garage and door. Scores of plants were strategically placed around the yard.

He slowed the car to a stop. "It is. It's been my favorite recent project. Do you want to stay in the car or come with me?" He searched her eyes for a clue as to what she was thinking. She glanced behind him, over his shoulder to the two men who were talking to each other by the large arched doorway.

"I want to come. But first, can you tell me who they are?" She gestured toward the men.

"The taller man with the buzz cut is my second-in-command. His name is Oliver Flournoy. He's a smooth-talking guy, but he's still single. The man he is talking to is Micah Segal, our CFO. Sometimes we go out with him and his wife, Brianna. They have a toddler, Danny. He adores you. Like all kids do."

"Okay. Oliver and Micah. Got it in here." She tapped her temple and let out a shaky laugh. She unclipped her seat belt and pushed herself out of the car so she could unbuckle Thomas.

Alaina really was something else. This was a huge step for her and seeing her step back into the world so fearlessly even in the face of her amnesia impressed him in a major way. She was an amazing woman, more than just beautiful. She had an inner strength that shone—and drew him. How had he lost sight of this side of her?

What a helluva time to want to tuck her away from prying eyes and kiss her until she sighed, and more.

He cleared his throat and his thoughts, narrowing his focus back on the moment at hand. By the time Thomas was out of his seat, Micah and Oliver were over at the car. Palpable silence descended on the group. Alaina rocked Thomas back and forth, eyes flicking from Oliver to Micah and back to Porter.

Oliver, a slim man with deep brown hair, cleared his throat to break the silence.

"How are you feeling, Alaina?" he asked, clearly feeling awkward as hell with her amnesia.

"Well. All things considered… And how are you, Oliver?"

"Doing well, doing well," he answered, repeating her polite words, bobbing his head. "Just gearing up for Christmas at my sister's."

"That's…good." She rocked Thomas, turning her attention to the shorter man with auburn hair. "And how are things with you, Micah?"

"No reason to complain, ma'am." He blinked fast as if forcing himself to make eye contact. "All's quiet and well at home."

More awkward silence descended. Damn. This was not going the way he'd thought it might.

"We are glad you are feeling better," Micah added. Blink, blink. Blink, blink.

"We are, too," Porter said, wishing he could say something to smooth things over. "Alaina, why don't you let me hold Thomas and you can go explore the grounds. The view from the back deck is stunning. Oliver, would you unlock the door for her?"

Alaina nodded, visibly relieved at the opportunity to escape. Brushing his hands along her arms, Porter took Thomas from her.

"Of course." Oliver unlocked the door and strode inside, flipping on lights. Alaina walked through the door frame, her movements quick and brisk. She was taking everything in. Seemed to love the driftwood-colored hardwood floors, the crisp white trim. She flashed Porter a quick smile over her shoulder before walking across the rooms to the patio door.

His eyes stayed on her a moment longer. He was struck by her bravery in facing this amnesia head-on, even when it wasn't easy. In the old days, he might have asked her about artwork for the place. Her expertise was always coveted by home buyers. He missed seeing the way her artist's mind worked. It had been one part of their marriage where they shared an easy accord.

"How are you handling the new kid? This fatherhood gig is something else." Micah made small talk with Porter as they moved through the house.

"It's everything I wanted and nothing I imagined." He would do anything for his son. Anything. He'd never expected to feel this much for another living being—the love, the protectiveness, the pride. "He's fun."

"And cute as hell." Micah tugged Thomas's healthy foot lightly. "How's his clubfoot healing? Gotta confess, I don't know a lot about this type of issue."

"He'll need two more surgeries and physical therapy, but the doctor expects a full recovery. I just hate that he has to hurt."

Micah nodded sympathetically. "He smiles when he sees you. That rocks."

"Truth." At least he had that going for him.

The bond he was already creating with his son made his heart swell. It made the dream of a family of his own more real—and more important.

"And Alaina?"

"She's a natural mother. No amnesia could steal that from her."

"I'm sorry, man. I wish I could say it's for the best, since y'all— Hell, that sounds insensitive."

Micah's features tensed. But Porter knew he didn't mean anything by the comment. Things had been so difficult before the accident. So rocky. It wasn't something they could keep hidden.

"Don't worry. I know you mean well." Their voices bounced around the skeleton of the house.

"Come have dinner with us. Let's hang out like old married couples." Micah's face showed genuine concern and interest. He was a good guy. The type Porter could always count on.

"I'll talk to Alaina. We'll see if she's up to it. She wants to talk to people from our past, and

I want to give her whatever she needs. We just have to tread carefully and follow the doctor's instructions." Porter explained a little of the situation to Micah, but his gaze moved to the side. Toward Alaina.

She was walking around the property, taking in the features of this house. She seemed to belong in the place. The softer, more classical lines and arches fit her better than the angles and modernism of their beach home.

Why hadn't he perceived this before? His mind filled with all the times she'd catered to his tastes and desires. He couldn't escape the realization that he needed to appreciate her for who she was, not just how she fit into his vision of the perfect family.

"Of course. Let's talk more and pick a time. Dinner at our place. Or a restaurant." Micah clapped him on the shoulder. "Or even go to the ballet."

"Seriously? The ballet?" Head cocking to the side, Porter snapped his attention back to the conversation.

"Just checking to be sure you're still listening. You were so busy staring at your wife."

It was hard not to stare at her. Alaina captivated his attention, his thoughts.

Seeing her in this house he wondered if surprising her with the beach house after finding out they would need fertility treatments a few years ago had been the right call. Should he have had her pick out a house with him instead? He'd cut her out of the decisions sometimes, telling himself he was surprising her. Yet then she was stuck pretending to be pleased.

He needed to set his mind on ways to fix that in the future, when he was considering major changes like remodeling or even relocation. Big changes he couldn't tackle right this second. But he could—and wanted—to do something special for her now, something she would like.

After they were back in the car, Porter started to drive toward a place they hadn't been to in ages. Fishin' Franks—her favorite restaurant. He wanted today to be special.

* * *

Lunch was absolutely delicious. Cajun fish tacos. Fresh avocados. Live music.

All things considered, Alaina was having a decent time being out of the beach house today. Porter was as charming as ever, completely sensitive to her every whim and desire. And to Thomas. Seeing them together made her heart surge. Porter was dedicated to the boy. Completely devoted to becoming a family.

For a moment, she considered what it would be like if her memories never came back.

Maybe this was all they needed. A completely fresh start. A new house for a new family. A house like the one at the job site. One that fed into her eclectic sensibilities and symbolized their new life together.

She could practically picture Thomas taking his first steps on the driftwood-colored hardwood floors. And art hanging all over the living room.

As they walked into the Baby Supplies Galore store, she scanned the faces of the other shoppers. In true Florida Christmas fashion, babies were dressed in shorts and tanks that sported flamingos in Santa hats.

The aisles were packed with late-December holiday shoppers. Christmas music mingled with the rush of families debating gifts.

Porter kept stride next to her as she pushed the cart down the least crowded aisle. His hand went almost instinctively to the small of her back. The warmth of his touch begged her to recall their past again. It clouded her sense of the present. Even knowing that they could be a family with a fresh start, she yearned to re-member what they'd shared.

"What was the best present you ever received from me for Christmas?" she asked, looking at the blanket sets.

Glancing at the prices, Alaina quickly realized this was a high-end baby store. Just one item probably cost as much as five of her childhood Christmases altogether. This was a completely different level of shopping.

"Hmm. There was one year that you did a

painting based on the blueprint of the building project that launched my career. I loved that. It's hanging above my desk in my office."

"I'd like to look at that more closely. Get an idea of the direction of my art. And what was my favorite Christmas present from you?"

"I think the best gift I ever gave you may have been the surprise trip to Paris. We spent a week in art galleries eating brie and bread."

"Ah, bread and cheese. Such a solid combination." She laughed to cover her regret that she couldn't remember what sounded like a beautiful trip. "What about your Christmases as a child?"

She slowed down beside a tower of holiday-themed baby rattles—penguins with red-and-green scarves, polar bears with fuzzy hats and deer with jingle bells.

"My mom went all out. Good God, she went all out. Mom's a lawyer. Did I tell you that?" He plucked a snowy owl out of a bin and waggled it in front of the baby, who rewarded him with a gummy grin.

"I don't believe anyone thought to tell me that detail, actually." She'd taken in so much information in such a short time it was hard to keep the facts straight. "I assumed she was independently wealthy. She took time off to be here? That's really sweet."

He waggled his hand. "Taking time off work is a way to put it, I guess. My mother sneaks off to work just like I do. Neither of us has ever been big on sleep."

"That's funny, given the impression she relays, snoozing in, preferring the baby be asleep."

"That's my mom. Contrary."

Alaina hugged a stuffed bear against the ache in her chest. "I wish my mother could be here to meet Thomas. She would love him."

His forehead furrowed with deep creases of concern. "I wish she could be here for you."

She set the bear back on the shelf, arranging him precisely. "Your mother's been surprisingly easy to get along with. This fresh start has been helpful perhaps. We don't feel threatened."

"You have no reason to feel threatened by my mother."

"She's certainly got it all together."

And what about her own life? Nothing about it felt together. A whole degree and career she couldn't remember participating in. What kind of exhibits had she been a part of?

There was no sense dwelling on it, though. Instead, she would put all of her energy into the present moment. Focusing on the past wasn't doing anyone any good. For now, she would worry about making Thomas's first Christmas something special.

Porter picked a reindeer and snowman ornament that read Baby's first Christmas. He flipped it over in his hand before handing it to Alaina. "What do you think of this one?"

She traced the ceramic ornament. "It's perfect. And speaking of firsts, since I haven't remembered anything, let's choose some new traditions to start today."

The fresh start she'd been daydreaming about could begin now.

"Such as?" he asked.

So many traditions to pick from. She opted for the simplest, one that connected so many families at the holidays. "Let's start with meals. What do we usually eat for Christmas?"

"Traditional turkey and a duck with all the trimmings. You like oyster stuffing so we have that. I like cranberry pie."

"While that sounds delicious, let's do away with it or eat it all on another day. For Christmas let's serve something totally different this year. A standing rib roast…" She snapped her fingers. "Or I know—how about we have a shrimp boil?"

"A shrimp boil? For Christmas?"

"Yes," she said, warming to the idea, feeling in control of the holiday and her new life for the first time. "In the Carolinas we call it frogmore stew, but down here it would be a shrimp boil. Shrimp, corn, new potatoes, maybe crawfish or crab or sausage in it, as well. We could have corn-bread stuffing, or crab and corn bread stuffing. What do you think?"

He held up a Santa hat and plopped it on her head. "I think you're so excited I'll eat anything if it makes you smile like that." His hand slid down to cup her face. "I've missed your smile."

Again, she thought about how he must feel in this situation. He'd lost his wife, for all intents and purposes. First to the coma and now to her inability to remember what they'd been to each other. And this certainly couldn't have been how he'd envisioned their first Christmas with their child. "I'm sorry for all the pain this is causing you."

"I'm not in pain right now. I'm happy. Really happy."

His eyes shone with sincerity that sent tingles into her stomach.

"Let's shop. This is one time I won't complain about all that money you have. Let's be Santa."

She pushed the cart forward to the next line of plush toys.

"I like the way you think. And I'm a sucker for stuffed animals." He tossed a giant polar bear at her. She caught it easily.

She waved it in front of Thomas, and even gave the bear a voice. Porter pulled down a small duck and started to play along with her.

It felt so natural. As if they were a normal family. As if they all belonged together. The baby giggled at the impromptu theater provided by his parents.

An elderly lady walked up to them. "If all parents were like you two, the world would be a wonderful place. You're giving that child the gift of imagination. It's lovely. What a beautiful family." The elderly lady grabbed a small teddy from the shelf.

"Thank you, ma'am." Porter rubbed his hand over Alaina's shoulder.

His hand sent her senses tingling. It had felt so natural. So perfect. Maybe there was a shot for them all after all.

"Merry Christmas. Y'all enjoy him while he's that small and adorable. Before you know it, he'll be a teenager asking for a car." She smiled at them and continued farther into the store.

"A car?" Porter chuckled, plucking up a rattle

shaped like a race car. "Easy enough for now. And clearly the polar bear and duck have to come home. They have Thomas's stamp of approval."

"I think you are right. I really like this elephant, too, though." She scooped the blue elephant off the shelf and her hand tightened.

The inky tendrils of a memory pushed into her mind. It felt as if she was underwater without goggles. It was unfocused at first. She and Porter at a friend's baby shower around the holidays. Laughing at the party. Overwhelmed with joy for their friends, for the baby that was about to come into their lives.

But knowing all the while that a baby wasn't about to enter her and Porter's life. How hard it was for them to go back home to their house on Christmas knowing they couldn't conceive. How much pain welled in her chest even now at the thought of that Christmas.

"What is it? What's wrong?" Porter asked, concern flooding his voice as he took the elephant from her.

The memory evaporated and she sank down, sitting on the edge of a display platform. "I just remembered something. From before. From a Christmas a few years ago, I'm not sure exactly when."

"Tell me," he insisted, kneeling beside her while keeping his hand securely on Thomas.

She struggled to remember every detail as if that might pry out more. "We went to a baby shower after finding out we couldn't conceive… I just…" Her voice trailed off. The words faded and closed in her throat.

"Shhh. It's okay." He wrapped an arm around her. Drew her close as ragged breaths escaped her throat. His embrace was somehow more familiar than the kiss, more real.

He stroked her back, murmured into her hair. This moment felt like the first thing she'd really shared with Porter since waking from the coma. And she sank into that feeling.

Would she be able to hang on to that once they returned home? Or would it evaporate like that ethereal memory?

<u>Six</u>

Porter had a knack for presentation and plans. It was a skill he'd picked up as he grew his construction empire. And it was something easily transferred to romance. He was a big-picture kind of guy.

And if any of his visions needed to pan out, it was this one.

The day after their shopping outing, he led Alaina through the house, hands covering her eyes.

"You swear you can't see?" His body pressed against hers as they shuffled forward. The light scent of her coconut shampoo wafted in the inches between them, making him remember the countless nights they'd spent together. How he wanted that now. Wanted her now.

But he had to put recovering their family first. Taking her to bed would jeopardize his plans since she didn't trust him yet.

"I swear. But what is all this about?"

"It's a surprise. You'll just have to trust me."

Damn. If that wasn't the statement of the moment. Trust him that the surprise was worth it. And that he was, too.

He spun her around the room, turning in circles until there was no doubt in his mind that she was completely disoriented.

Two turns later, and they were in the family room. Dropping his hands, he waited while she surveyed the room and the additions he'd purchased just for her.

A ten-foot-tall live Christmas tree stood centered in the three bay windows. It was already lit, the white lights bathing the room in a warm glow.

Two boxes of decorations—special ordered

and newly delivered—were stacked on the white-and-tan-striped couch, pushed up against the blue pillows of embroidered crabs and starfish. The shelving unit behind the couch had been emptied of the normal knickknacks of lighthouses, shells and boats.

A blank canvas. Perfect for making new memories. And maybe uncovering other old ones that would bring them closer together. Of course there was also the risk that she would remember the wrong ones. That she would realize how close they'd come to divorcing and wonder why he hadn't told her.

This was how they would build a family together. She had been right earlier. It was time to start creating family traditions. Ones Thomas would grow into.

Traditions grounded a person, gave them a firm foundation to build a life upon, and clearly Alaina had a gift for that he hadn't recognized before. Maybe because he'd been too busy trying to wedge her into his preconceived notions of a family portrait rather than letting them make it together.

He wanted to create the family he'd never had as a kid. It was always just him, his mom and whatever guy she was pursuing at the time. There had been no long-standing traditions on Christmas or any other time. He loved his mother, of course, but they were distant. And he wanted better for his son.

He'd always wanted this. It was why he'd grabbed this second chance. But he was starting to see he'd sacrificed some of Alaina's preferences to reach his goal.

"How did you get this here so quickly?" Gesturing to the boxes and the tree. Blue eyes dancing in the muted light.

"The idea came to me while we were shopping and I had it all delivered."

"But you already had the decorations in place for when we arrived."

"Those were the ones here before, the ones outside and in the living room. It struck me today we didn't have anything less formal, for us as a family here, to open gifts with Thomas."

She hugged him hard. "Thank you, it's perfect." Then she froze, stepping back and turning away fast to dig around in the box closest to them. She lifted the decorations out and stacked them on the coffee table in front of the couch.

"Did I choose those others in the main living room? They don't seem like me." She shot him a look. "They're so…matchy…modern art deco rather than the smoother Renaissance palettes I gravitate toward."

"You're right." And he was seeing how he'd missed the mark and wished that he'd paid more attention. "Most of the decorations came with the house. I bought the place as a gift to you."

"You didn't build this?" Surprise cut into her voice as she lifted the palm tree crèche out of the box. Leaning against the space between the boxes on the couch, she placed the crèche on the center shelf.

"Oh, I did. But for another family. They had everything in place, ready to move in and then

they split up. I picked up the place for a song…
um…not that I wouldn't have spent a fortune
for you." A sheepish grin pulled on his cheeks.
He placed a running silver reindeer on the low-
est shelf behind the couch.

"I know that. Clearly."

Was that a dig? Was she complaining about
their lifestyle? He shook off the defensiveness
and thought about her, her wants and preferences, and recalled how uncomfortable she'd always been with his wealth. "We always planned
to redecorate and never got around to it. I should
have insisted."

"Or I should have insisted. I'm an adult. I
take responsibility for decisions I made, even
if I can't remember them." She rolled her eyes.

"Would you like to redo the whole place? Or
our primary residence?"

"Primary residence? Hmmm. That still feels
so…surreal. Like everything else in my life."
She toyed with a red satin bow. "I haven't even
seen our regular house in Tallahassee yet. Is it
like this?"

"No, you had carte blanche there."

"How long have we lived in that house?" She sat on the tile floor between the couch and the coffee table with the box of new tree ornaments in front of her. Each one unique and made by a local artisan. Reaching into the box she began to remove all kinds of ornaments. It was a mismatched set. She set them down, one by one, on the coffee table, eyes sharp with obvious approval.

He thought back to those early days when they'd had so much hope for their future, planning a big family, children, grandchildren, growing old together. "We had it built when we got married."

"So we made those decisions together."

"We did." Kneeling, he helped her take the remaining ornaments out of the box. He lifted the first ornament they'd ever got together as newlyweds: two penguins on a snowbank holding hands. Gently, he set it next to the ornament that sported a snowman made of sand.

"I wish we'd gone to our house first." Her

fingers roved gently over top of all the decorations. It was as if she was trying to gain memories by osmosis. She stopped over a Santa Claus ornament. He was posed in a Hawaiian shirt and board shorts, and he had a pink flamingo beneath his hands. A small laugh escaped her lips and she brought the Santa to the tree and hung it on a bough.

"We still can." He brought a snowflake ornament with him and hung it slightly below hers.

"But we're settled for now and have the follow-up appointments with Thomas's doctor. After Christmas we can settle into a new routine."

"It's a lot to take in at once, both places."

"That's perceptive of you."

They kept bringing ornaments to the tree, filling the boughs until they grew heavy with their collective past. He enjoyed the way that she laughed over the ornaments. The way each one was an act of discovery for her.

The evening was too good to be true.

Just as they were getting ready to put the

angel on top of the tree, his mother's laughter floated into the room a second before she entered, hanging on the arm of a man with salt-and-pepper hair.

She waved her son over. "Come here, darling. You too, Alaina."

What the hell? Porter pushed to his feet and silently fumed. Who was this man? Didn't his mother realize they needed a calm and quiet family holiday? Her surprise visit had already added enough additional chaos to the equation.

"Mom, what's going on?"

"I want you to meet my new friend Barry. He's a tax attorney."

Now that seemed right. He was as polished as she was.

Barry thrust out his hand. "Nice to meet you both. Your mom has been telling me a lot about you." His grip was tight as he shook Porter's hand. "Oh, you're putting up another tree? Best part of the whole Christmas season if you ask me."

The guy was nice enough. Smooth. But so

were most attorneys. They knew how to read people and work a room. This guy was no exception.

"I feel the same way, Barry." Alaina's voice cut his thoughts in half.

Courtney hugged Barry's arm closer. "I'm so glad he's joining us for dinner tonight. It'll be a little party."

"Mother, I need to talk to you. Mind if I show you something?" And with that he hooked Courtney's arm in his. Smiling tightly, he led her out of the family room and into the hallway.

He glanced back into the room to see his mother's newest suit-of-a-boyfriend helping Alaina put the angel on the tree. Something he had wanted to do with her. Damn it. Who pushed in on someone else's Christmas decorating?

"Mom," he hissed softly, "did you have to bring your boyfriend over now? Alaina's condition is delicate and we have a new baby."

"First—" she held up a slim finger "—Alaina is stronger than you give her credit for. Second, your child is asleep. And third, he's not my boyfriend. We just met at a local fund-raiser I was attending at the invitation of your neighbor Sage."

How freaking perfect. Sage was up to her usual tricks. She'd probably invited his mother to glean some information about what was going on with Alaina. She'd use their struggle as gossip at the next society function.

"There's a helluva lot going on here without adding strangers to the mix. You should have spoken to me."

"Let me get this straight." His mother folded her arms. "I showed up uninvited and brought my uninvited pickup. That makes you uncomfortable."

Always the lawyer. Even out of the courtroom.

"You're leading the witness, Mother."

"Fair enough." She held up both hands. "Barry and I will go out."

He gave an exasperated sigh as he put his hand to the back of his neck. "No, stay. It'll only be more awkward if you haul him back out after announcing he's staying for dinner."

She clacked away from him, back into the great room, heading to the last box of Christmas decorations.

So much for creating stable traditions and experiences like a normal family. Tonight was supposed to have been calm. Relaxing. A night for him and Alaina to grow closer. To move toward becoming a family. Turns out that was just as difficult for him as it was for her.

Alaina cut through her petite filet with ease. Shoveling a forkful into her mouth, she watched the verbal volleyball tournament between her mother-in-law and Porter. The tension in the room rolled in waves.

"I'm just saying, sweetie, that if you move the Christmas tree closer to the fireplace in the family room, there will be enough room for us to sit comfortably and display all of Thomas's gifts." Courtney used her fork to slice up the asparagus before continuing. "Think of how visually appealing that will be. Think of the pictures of Thomas's first Christmas. You only get one first Christmas, you know."

Porter set down his crystal water goblet. "Yes, Mother, that is true, but—"

"But what? You're not worried about the pictures. Believe me, you'll regret that in a few years."

Porter let out a deep sigh, and speared a piece of his medium rare steak with his silver fork. His face remained calm, but Alaina noticed the way his jaw flexed. It was a small movement but it was there and had nothing to do with eating his meal.

"So, Barry—" Alaina broke into the conversation in an attempt to let the heat fade "—have you always lived in Florida?"

"No, no. Though I have been here for forty years, so it seems funny to claim another state when I've acquired the Florida tan we all get from simply walking around. I'm actually from Colorado originally. Just outside of Denver.

Have you ever been there?" Barry sipped his wine, eyes as keen as the cut crystal.

Such a simple question. Yet panic filled her. Had she been to Colorado? That was the tricky part about conversations with strangers.

"Oh, Barry, you can't put Alaina on the spot like that right now." Courtney chimed in, touching his arm. "She was a victim of a terrible car accident. She's got a mild case of amnesia."

Porter pinned Courtney with a glare. She merely blinked in response. Alaina's eyes slid from Courtney to Porter. While it was true, she didn't like the ill effects of her accident being casually brought into conversation. So she decided to take charge of this conversation.

"By mild amnesia, my mother-in-law means I've forgotten the past five years." Alaina tapped her fingernail on her water glass. "Other than that, I'm fine and prefer people not treat me with kid gloves."

"All right, then," Barry agreed. "I can understand that—"

Courtney stopped him with another touch to

the arm. "It's just easier if people know what they are dealing with up front. They get a fact pattern and suddenly, they understand how to handle a situation."

"Spoken like a true lawyer. Give me the facts." Barry wheezed out a laugh.

Porter's jaw flexed again. His disapproval of the way his mother had introduced the life-changing accident was more than apparent. Alaina could tell that any second now, he might explode, and that was the last thing she wanted or needed. Not to mention their reactions confused her. What was with all this tension? What was she missing—well, other than five years. So much of her life was confusing.

But right now wasn't about her. It was about her husband, who was clearly upset. She reached under the table to touch his knee, squeezing lightly until he looked at her. She pleaded with her eyes and somehow he seemed to understand.

Was this what it was like to be married? Was this an almost memory, the way they could communicate without words? It felt good.

"Amnesia, huh," Barry said between bites of his dinner. "That's rotten luck, Alaina. I wish you a speedy recovery."

"Thanks. I'm lucky to have such a great support system here." It was the most diplomatic answer she could manage. She gave Porter's knee another quick squeeze of thanks. And then returned her attention to her filet.

From the other end of the room, Thomas erupted in a gut-wrenching cry.

Alaina and Porter both sprang to their feet and rushed to the jungle-themed baby swing. She eased Thomas out and up, cradling him in her arms, rocking him back and forth. He still fussed.

"He's hungry," she said, glancing down at her watch. It was definitely dinnertime.

"I've got it." Porter's murmur was low, almost too soft to hear. Porter left the dining room and jogged into the kitchen. Moments later, he re-emerged with a burp cloth and bottle, already a seasoned pro at this dad thing.

How long had they wanted this?

A whispery memory rippled through her mind of her looking at Porter as he held an infant swaddled in blue. But the baby boy wasn't Thomas—somehow she knew it was the son of Porter's CFO, the boy who was now a toddler.

Her heart ached to see the longing in his face, and then the memory faded, the rest gone. She swallowed down the lump in her throat and looked at her husband, the man still so new to her now but who had felt so familiar in the memory.

Courtney set her Waterford wineglass down on the table, half rising from her chair to get a better look at them. "Don't you have a live-in nurse to take care of him, Porter?"

"I just want to make sure I'm there for my son and that he knows who I am." He tested the milk on his wrist, then handed it to Alaina.

"And you are, Porter." Courtney dabbed at the corners of her mouth. "But you hired help. So let them help. You don't need to hover. I certainly never hovered over you and I was a single parent. I wouldn't steer you wrong. Not when it comes to my grandson."

"I appreciate that, Mother." Porter's tone was level as if he knew to keep it calm for his son, although the set of his broad shoulders made it clear his patience with his mother was nearing an end. "But I think a mix of help and hands-on work is best. Besides, we won't use the help forever. That's just until we've settled back into a routine."

So he had been serious when he'd said the night nurse was a component of her recovery. He was sincere about being a fully involved parent. She admired that. Wanted to be part of that unit. Thomas deserved that dedication from both of them.

His mom's counter came within seconds. "That's where I think you might be wrong. I think the full-time help is wonderful. It really expands what you can do at the company. You know he's in good hands. And you can work more, grow the empire and make sure he has whatever he wants in his life."

Alaina assumed her mother-in-law's advice was coming from a good place. But it seemed more than a tad controlling. She admired Porter's restraint in not calling out his mom on that and wondered if he was holding back to keep things peaceful, not just for Thomas, but for Alaina, too.

Maybe this had been why she and her mother-in-law hadn't gotten along before the amnesia. She didn't need her memories to clue her in on *that*.

She just resented the way Porter's and his mother's issues were intruding on what had been the best day Alaina could remember having with her husband, when there were precious few to remember.

In spite of knowing there was so much of her life left to uncover, she found herself wanting more of those new memories.

He closed the door behind his mother. Finally. And not soon enough.

He'd known this was a bad idea, having his

mom here for Christmas. She hadn't ever been the home and hearth for the holidays sort, and she certainly hadn't got along with Alaina. This wasn't the joyous, peaceful atmosphere he'd been attempting to create with his wife. This evening was a prime example. His day with Alaina had been derailed by that damn awkward dinner.

At least Courtney was out for the evening with Barry the tax attorney. Just like that, she'd become the mother of his youth. The one who was interested in men more than family. The one who put boyfriends first.

Alaina's misfortune was that she couldn't remember a thing. His great curse was that he couldn't forget a single damn moment. What a pair they made.

Cricking his neck to the side, he strode to his office computer and uploaded some videos of their Tallahassee house onto a disc for Alaina so she could see where they'd lived. Maybe that would jostle a memory. And maybe she would see her own stamp on their life in a way she hadn't here.

He was struck by the irony. Even with streaming music, some people still made music mixes on CDs as a gift, full of "their songs." Not him. But then he wasn't sure she would even like the same music anymore. His whole life felt upside down lately.

He thought all he'd wanted was the family he'd dreamed of having, but in getting to know Alaina again, seeing her in a new way after the accident, his feelings were mixed up.

Even his mother's behavior tonight had rocked him. It's not that he minded that she had a new beau. She was a grown-up, after all. But it brought the weight of his past crashing down on him.

Needing to calm himself, Porter made his way to Thomas's nursery. Seeing his son was a way to remind himself that this was not the past. That he was going to be an active part of his son's life. That he was making the family he'd always wanted.

Porter had never lacked material objects as a child. His mother was a brilliant attorney and made a decent salary.

But he had been profoundly lonely. And he never wanted Thomas to experience that. Never wanted him to feel as if he wasn't welcome, as if he wasn't wanted.

Courtney had chased love for Porter's whole life. Moving from man to man. Men who seldom bothered to learn Porter's name, always settling on the generic "sport" or "son." Nameless. Invisible.

He'd attended an elite boarding school from middle school through high school. He was home for three weeks over Christmas and two months over the summer.

It was common for his mother to promise to spend time with him only to bail in favor of a date and time at the bar. She'd always promised to take him to movie releases, or ice-skating or bowling. But more often than not, Porter did all those things with a nanny instead of with his mother. He was frequently sent to his room so his mother and her current boyfriend could have the run of the house, child-free.

But there had been one Christmas break when he was in seventh grade that completely changed their relationship forever. It was part of the reason he still felt so distant from his mother. The experience left him feeling like a part-time son in a part-time family.

Alaina might not have ever gone to Colorado, but he sure as hell had.

He had come home from break, excited for the plans he had made with his mother over the school year. They were supposed to go skiing in Colorado. It was going to be a winter wonderland filled with snow, hot chocolate and sports.

They had gone to Colorado. But Courtney had brought a nanny along for the ride. As well as her boyfriend. She'd enrolled Porter in a snow camp for the day and the nanny entertained him at night while Courtney wined and dined. He'd even discovered she planned the whole trip around her meet-up with the guy. Porter had felt completely let down. He'd wanted to spend time with his mother. Even as a teen, he'd been seeking that connection. But it was on that trip that he'd realized it would never happen. If he wanted a family of his own, he would have to create it himself.

Shoving the memory aside, Porter stood over the crib. Thomas snoozed, breathing light little breaths. He was so peaceful.

It would be different for Thomas. Porter and Alaina would figure out how to be around each other. They would move past the temporary truce they'd erected before the accident and live as a family. Alaina seemed to feel their connection as much as he did. Even if she regained her memories, surely she would forgive the past and stay this time. And they both already felt so bonded to their son.

A muted knock sounded from behind him. Porter wheeled around to see Alaina standing in the doorway. She'd already changed for bed. She was in a racerback tank top that showed off her ample curves. The black shorts hugged her legs, inching up her strong thighs. His gaze lingered on her smiling face.

"Hey. You know, today was pretty amazing. Maybe you're not so terrible at that romance thing." Her voice was low, but playful. Almost like the Alaina he had first fallen in love with. He ached to grab her, to draw her into his arms.

"Well, I only know how to go big or go home."

"Today was great. All the things we found for Thomas. You bringing the decorations out for us tonight. Trying to get our own holiday traditions started. It was sweet and it meant a lot to me." She stepped close to him. Just barely out of reach.

Close enough that the coconut scent of her shampoo teased his senses. Close enough that he ached to pull her to him and take her to bed. Patience be damned. But there was too much at stake. Keeping them together. Keeping her happy. Keeping her.

He forced himself to measure his words.

"I want us to be a family." He stuffed his hands into his pockets to keep from grabbing her and saying to hell with talking. "And I think your idea of a shrimp boil is a great follow-up to what we did tonight. We are a team. Input from both of us matters."

"I think so, too. The time we're spending here is helping." She paused, her beautiful blue eyes glazing over with her attempt at looking inward. "I also vaguely recall making the painting I gave you. I can see it in my mind. It's a bit fuzzy, but I can remember the colors I used, the brushes…"

Memories. He should be rejoicing. And he *was* glad for her, but he couldn't stop the impending sense of doom. What would happen when she remembered all the mistakes he'd made? When she realized those were the questions he had avoided answering?

"It's great that you're starting to remember. I love your paintings. Your colors. I can't wait for you to re-see our house in Tallahassee."

He just prayed they could mend their marriage—their family—before the rest came rolling in. The bad parts. The possible divorce.

And God—that sucker punched him. The stakes were higher than ever. They had a child now and Porter felt he was getting to know Alaina all over again.

"What other kinds of things did you give me over the years? You know, aside from a beautiful beach house?" Leaning over the crib, she rearranged the baby blanket.

"The humanities, art specifically, is clearly important to you. In Tallahassee, you're extremely active in the Art Association. And you wanted elementary school kids to be exposed to art. So I started a scholarship program in your name that brings artists into the classroom."

"Porter, that's so generous of you. I don't know what to say."

Her face flushed with such gratitude he felt guilty for keeping other facts from her. Facts about their marriage. But he was focused on the bigger picture, a long-term answer for them. Their future as a family. She would see that, if she suddenly remembered everything. She had to.

"You don't have to thank me, Alaina. You deserve it. And the program has been a success. The kids really benefit from it."

She looked at him them. Really and truly looked at him. He held her gaze, reading the warmth in her sky-blue eyes. The eyes of his wife and the eyes of a stranger at the same time.

Thomas began to stir, making little clucking noises. Poor guy. They were disturbing his much-needed sleep.

"I think we might be too loud."

"I guess that's our cue. We've got to let sleeping babies sleep." He took the monitor so he could give it to the matronly night nurse. "Besides, there is one more surprise for you. But it's back downstairs."

Alaina followed him back down the stairs and into the family room. They didn't bother with the actual light, but chose to sit beneath the glow of the Christmas tree.

"Close your eyes." His whisper tickled her

ear. She let her eyes flit shut. A box was placed gently in her lap.

"All right. You can open them. And the present." Porter sat across from her, on the ground. Eyeing the box, she tore into the perfectly wrapped package. She lifted the flap.

And gasped in delight and breathed in the scent. Her soul sang.

Canvas paper. Acrylic paint. Oil paint. Chalk. Paintbrushes and sketching pencils. Everything she needed for a quick art set.

"Oh, Porter. You didn't have to...I mean...you could have waited for Christmas..." Her voice hitched in her throat. Emotions pulsed. Her breathing sped up in anticipation. She couldn't wait to pour out her emotions on the page.

He cupped her shoulders. "I'm a pretty simple guy. I want my family to have what they want. What they need. And I thought it would be a good outlet for you. I think this is the longest you've ever gone without some creative project."

In the deepest part of her being, she was truly

touched. He had been trying so hard to connect with her. To do things to make her feel more comfortable. Even if their life before the accident hadn't been perfect, the man before her now was putting in a real effort.

"Porter, it's perfect. Thank you." She grabbed his hand, beginning to feel as if she knew the texture and feel of him. He tucked her hair behind her ear.

"Of course."

"Can I ask another question?"

"Always."

"How did we decide on the name Thomas?" It had been her father's name. She hoped that had been the reason, but she didn't trust much about her instincts these days. A pang of sorrow shot through her. Her father would never know her son. She took a shaky breath. His loss felt so recent.

Porter inched toward her. They were side by side. His shoulder brushed hers and she leaned into him. Breathed in the dark clove scent of his cologne.

"We chose the name for your father. It wasn't much of a discussion. I never had a father and your father sounded wonderful even if I never had the honor of meeting the guy. It seemed right. Fitting." He wrapped his arm around her, and she buried her face in his chest. The tightness of his arm on hers ramped up her heartbeat. He was beginning to feel like someone she could talk to. Trust was still an iffy idea, but she was moved by his actions today.

She couldn't deny it. She was ready to take this to the next step. She craved intimacy with him. Her body ached for him, recognizing him on an instinctive level that went beyond memories.

"I know there must have been difficulties between us. Probably a strain because of the infertility," she began to say. She had to finish before she lost her nerve. "And probably a bunch of other things that I don't need to know right now…but I'm glad that we are trying to become a family now. And I was wondering if you could stay the night with me. Just sleeping. Nothing else. What do you think?"

His eyebrows shot upward. "I think I would be an idiot to say no."

Seven

Alaina couldn't believe she'd asked to share a bed with her husband. Not sex. Just sleeping.

She stood in her bathroom, changing into the pajamas she'd chosen. Choosing them had been tough. What to wear to sleep with a man she was attracted to, but wasn't ready to have sex with? If she wore a nightgown or a T-shirt, that would invite his hand to tunnel upward.

If she wore something silky, then that would feel like skin, sexy. But she didn't want to be frumpy. She couldn't help but feel vain in wanting to look attractive for her husband. So she'd opted for colors that flattered her. A pale pink tank top, cotton but thin. And a striped pair of shorts, so yes, their legs could brush.

Because she wanted this. Needed this, to be close to another human being. To her husband. Some part of her body knew they'd been together. Often. For a long time. There was a synchronicity in the way they moved through life that spoke of having done things together as a team, everyday things, sexual things.

When she'd first woken up from her coma, she'd felt as if the past five years hadn't existed. That it had only been a few months since she'd broken off her relationship with Douglas and taken out a restraining order.

But during the week in the hospital and then the week at the beach house, she had gained a sense of distance from the past. These weeks had helped ease the initial tension that had made her feel stuck in another time.

Had she moved beyond all those awful feelings left over from Douglas? She must have, since she'd got married. Even with her memories of the past five years gone, her sense of

Douglas felt further away than when she'd first woken up in the hospital. It was as if her body was moving forward to absorb the lost time even if her brain didn't fill in the missing pieces.

Her past with Porter hadn't returned, but her feelings for him were definitely growing. Strong. Real.

Powerful.

She looked down at her engagement ring and the wedding band. For the first time, she felt as if maybe, just maybe, they fit.

When Porter had given her those art supplies, she'd felt connected to him. She'd been given a link to her past with those supplies in hand. It made her want to find more links to the past, make more connections. It made her want this night with her husband.

She tugged on her pj's, the soft cotton brushing against her breasts and sending a shiver of awareness through her.

This wasn't going to be as easy as she'd thought.

Deep breath in. One foot in front of the other. She could do this.

The bedroom was washed in warm yellow light from the oversize candle emblazoned with an anchor on the mahogany dresser. It cast flickers on the ship steering wheel that leaned from dresser to wall.

Matchy-matchy. Maybe she would try her hand at redecorating this place. Make it feel less like a page out of a catalog and more like a home for a family always on the go. But she'd only make those decisions with Porter. Joint decisions. Like the decisions they had made earlier today with Thomas's gifts.

Porter slouched against the door frame, half looking at her. His black sweatpants hung low on his hips. A white T-shirt for a local Tallahassee baseball team enhanced his athletic frame. Damn, he was sexy.

And he was hers.

Alaina toyed with the band on her shorts. "This is a little awkward."

"I'm sorry you feel that way."

"Me, too, but I said it, and then I couldn't take it back."

"You don't have to."

She took a deep breath. "I think I do." She yanked back the covers, then paused, inhaling hard. "I don't even know what side of the bed I sleep on."

"You're fine," he said.

"Are you saying that to be accommodating? Or is that the truth?"

"The truth. Your instincts are right. That's your side of the bed."

Something eased inside her. Maybe she needed to follow her instincts more with him.

Alaina climbed into bed and patted the space beside her. "Okay. Join me."

He lay on top of the spread. "Done, as requested."

"And I didn't die."

"Wow, now that's a turn-on."

Laughing, she shoved him gently with both hands and felt the resistance in his muscles as her skin met his. He let out a low chuckle, clearly amused.

She sagged back into the fluffy feather pillow. He reclined on his side, propping his head on his hand.

Alaina picked at the down comforter. "What's next? Our situation is so unconventional I don't know what the rules are."

"No rules as far as I'm concerned. We're making this up as we go."

Still, she wanted details, a sense of who'd they'd been. "How did we used to sleep? Did I sleep on your chest? Did we spoon? Me against you? You against me? Opposite sides of bed?"

"Why don't we just see where we end up?" He held out an arm.

After only an instant's hesitation, she rested her head on his shoulder and his arm wrapped around her. A sigh filled her. This. This was right. The feel of her body fitting against her husband's.

Sleep pulled at her eyelids. It had been an exhausting day. Being here with Porter felt so damn right. Familiar. As if by muscle memory, her body curled around him, and she took comfort in the steady rise and fall of his broad chest.

Her eyelids fluttered shut. How was it possible to be entirely at ease and so on edge all at once?

Sleep was the furthest thing from Porter's mind.

Then again, that was nothing new. Not since the accident. Since the endless blur of days and nights at the hospital. He'd taken to doing work in the odd hours of the evening. Using work as a way to keep his mind off the dire situation of his family.

But tonight, he was working for different reasons. He needed to keep himself occupied, to keep his hands off his wife. Tonight, concentration was difficult. Near impossible, with Alaina pressed against him.

It had been so damn long since he'd held her like this. Since the warmth of her body melted with his. He absently ran a hand through her hair. She drew in closer.

How had it been so long since they'd done this? Been in bed together, nestled against each other.

Too long.

Yes, he wanted to touch her, to make love to her, but he had to keep his goals in mind. For the first time in months, he felt as if they were working together. That they were in this for real. Not just him, but her, too. They were becoming a family. At least, he thought they were. His own experiences with family were shaky at best. And her family was gone. But *this* family—this family had a shot.

He returned his attention back to his tablet. Looked over some reports. Started to feel the pull of sleep.

But something was wrong. Alaina started to shake. She twisted away from him.

"Stop it." Her voice was a murmur. But there was desperation in it.

"Let go. Just…just. No. Stop." Her lovely face contorted with fear. She continued to thrash against an invisible assailant.

She was having a nightmare.

Gently, he shook her shoulder. "Alaina. You're okay. You're okay."

She gasped in air. Her blue eyes suddenly alert. Scanning the room. Focusing on him. Breathing rapidly, her body twitchy. "I'm sorry. I didn't mean to wake you. Oh, God, this plan isn't working out like I meant it… I should just go."

He clasped her arm. "Stay. Do you remember what you dreamed? Did you recall something from the past?"

"No, not really." She sagged back against him. "I was just having a nightmare about Douglas, about that time with him. Things get muddled in dreams, feeling out of control and scared. Did I tell you about Douglas?"

"Your ex-boyfriend before you met me? Yes, you did."

"What did I tell you?"

"Are you trying to pull information out of me? Have you forgotten parts of that time in your life, too?"

"I remember. He was verbally abusive. I didn't see that for a long time. Then he hit me..." She shook her head. "And then I was done. I walked out."

"That's what you told me." Once he'd learned about the jerk, Porter had made a point to keep tabs on the guy, make sure he honored that restraining order. "I'm sorry tonight is bringing back bad memories for you. This was supposed to be a positive experience."

"It would have been worse if I'd been alone. Let's try again."

"I'd like that, too." She maneuvered into the crook of his arm. Laid a hand on his chest. He pulled her tightly against him, his mind churning with ways to help her feel at ease, to know he wouldn't let anything happen to her. Her breathing slowed, falling into the rhythmic pattern of a deep sleep.

And even with the determination to keep her safe from threats like Douglas, and to keep his hands to himself until she was ready for more,

Porter couldn't deny he had no way to keep her safe from thoughts of the past.

The yellow-orange rays of dawn's first light filtered in between the tulle-like curtains, nudging Alaina awake. She glanced over at her husband, whose eyes were still closed, heavy with sleep.

Quietly, she slid from bed and crept down the hall to check on the baby.

Thomas greeted her with a chubby-cheeked smile.

"Are you hungry, my love?" she cooed, picking him up out of bed. She sat with him in the rocker while he drank from the bottle. This was her favorite time of the day, just the two of them alone. She fed him and rocked him even though he was awake. She talked to him and sang to him. Time passed in a vacuum, a couple of hours sliding by in a beautiful haze.

This was everything she'd always hoped motherhood would be. A calmness descended on her as she sat with Thomas. And a desire to crawl back into bed with Porter. To memorize all of his features. To hold these moments close so they couldn't slip away like the others.

Maybe it was time to start drawing again. A family portrait. She'd start with Porter. Capture the angles of his face, the strength in his chest. And the smile lines in his face. And somehow, maybe their years together would come rushing back as she revisited him.

After finishing with Thomas, she set him down for a nap. Kissed his forehead. Filled with love for the making of her little family. She'd sketch him next.

On tiptoe, she made her way downstairs, grabbed her new sketchbook and pencils and crawled back into bed. Sunlight streamed over Porter's face.

She began to outline him. Rough strokes on paper. She worked first on his face. She started to lose herself in the drawing, the world ebbing away from her.

Until a knock sounded from behind her. Alaina practically leaped out of her skin.

"Sleeping Beauty's still asleep, I see." Her mother-in-law called from the door, a diamond-

and-silver snowflake broach pinned to the collar of her shirt. Porter let out a loud snore and turned on his side.

"Have breakfast with me? I could use some toast. And girl time." She motioned for Alaina to follow her down the hall.

"Sounds great. I am a bit hungry myself." Alaina stacked her sketchbook and pencils on the bedside table. If she stayed here much longer, she might not be able to resist temptation. She needed some space to gather her thoughts—and her mother-in-law might well have insights that could help her decide how to move forward in the marriage.

She hurried after Courtney into the hallway toward the back stairway leading to the kitchen.

When she'd caught up to her mother-in-law, Courtney glanced over her shoulder on her way down the steps. "I've never seen you draw before. You know, you get the same look on your face as Porter does when he is working on a building design."

"I do?"

She nodded, clasping the polished steel railing. "Porter's always been a hands-on guy. Started back in middle school. He was always building things. Once, he built a table for me for Christmas. He was sixteen then. Said he'd loved the sweat equity of the project. The ability to create something from nothing. I guess that's a bit like art, isn't it?"

"I suppose it's actually a similar process. Built not bought. I think that's why this house feels foreign to me. It's cookie cutter decor in a lot of ways other than some of the artwork. I'll take some imperfections in my decorations if it's coming from scratch."

"You sound like him. When he built that table, I think that's when he decided he didn't need me anymore." Courtney gave a slight laugh. But the sound was tinged with sadness.

They turned the corner into the kitchen and sat on the bar stools facing a view of the water, where a holiday boat parade was organizing. Festively decorated boats of all sizes congregated. A blow-up Santa in a bathing suit sat on the deck of one, but most of the vessels were outfitted more simply with green garland boughs.

"I'm sure he still needed you then. You helped shape him into the person he is today." A person she was still trying to understand. To relearn.

Her mother-in-law's eyebrows arched as she popped two slices of bread in the toaster. "Sometimes I wonder. He's built every house he's lived in as an adult. Sometimes I'm surprised he didn't build the yacht, too."

Alaina said, "Whoa, wait. We own one of those yachts?"

"You do. Usually my son has me stay out there rather than in the house, which, quite frankly, is an amazing spin on a mother-in-law suite. But still. We've always had troubles, my son and I."

Her mother-in-law straightened the rings on her fingers before she continued. "You know, I was madly in love with Porter's father. I was young—and the whole world seemed open to me when we were together. But he had other dreams. Other desires. He left shortly after Porter was born."

"I'm sure that was difficult. Raising Porter alone and working so much."

"Would you like the truth, Alaina? I was—and still am—brilliant in the courtroom. I can dissect a case like nobody's business. But motherhood? That never came to me. Not like it does to you."

Alaina nodded sympathetically, but didn't say anything. She knew Courtney had her quirks, but she never doubted that the woman loved her son. Family was just complicated. Alaina felt as if she knew that better than anyone. Funny what a few weeks in a coma had done for her perspective.

Porter was a man whom she was only just beginning to understand. But the tension between her husband and mother-in-law was starting to make sense to her. Courtney was all about buying premade items. It's why she'd insisted on the night nurse tending to Thomas.

But Porter—Porter was a man intent on creation. On actively building. He'd built a construction empire the same way he'd built that table. To prove he could take scraps and turn them into something usable. He'd built his life from the ground up, even though he could have easily used his mother's fortune. He hadn't backed down from the work it required.

And what about her? Alaina had spent the past two weeks in the haze of amnesia. Afraid of what she'd find if she pressed too hard. But Porter was aware of their history. Aware of their struggles. And he was still dedicated to their family. Maybe she needed to become aware, too.

And that meant digging around in the dirt a bit. And possibly talking to Sage.

As Alaina poured two cups of coffee in holiday mugs painted with angels, she made up her mind. Today was a day for exploring. And she would start with all the pieces of her past—even the uncomfortable ones. The time had come to reconstruct her life.

Starting with finding out more about how and why they'd purchased that yacht when she could have sworn such flashy purchases weren't her style.

Eight

Porter was still stunned over Alaina suggesting they go out to the yacht. He couldn't recall her ever suggesting that. In fact, the eighty-foot *Sunseeker* had been a contentious issue between them since he'd bought it two years ago. But he wasn't turning his back on the chance to get closer to her.

In the past, she'd always hated the vessel. Said it was too showy. Too flashy. It screamed their wealth, and that bothered her down to the core.

But Porter had never felt that way about the purchase. To him, it represented freedom. A chance to leave the world behind. To be completely untethered from the responsibilities of work and reliant on himself. And yes, he'd hoped it would offer them more time to relax together, bring them closer as their marriage began to fray.

The Florida winter sun warmed him. The captain had dropped anchor and gone into town about a half hour ago. The luxury craft happily rocked with the waves and the current, other boats far enough away to give him and Alaina a sense of privacy he welcomed. Water lapped against the sides and a healthy breeze coated the deck. They'd intended to take Thomas with them, but his mother had offered to watch him. She had even insisted. Though they did hire a backup sitter for all the tasks Courtney was not enthusiastic about performing.

He'd come out of the cabin with two bottles of water. One for him and one for Alaina.

Every day he was feeling closer to her, closer than he could remember feeling before. They were building something, a new connection. And since last night he felt a change between them. Something that had been missing for a long time before the accident.

He took a moment to appreciate her. Just the way she was in this moment. She'd dressed in layered tank tops and leggings, flip-flops half on, half off. She was sprawled on the white cushioned deck chair. Hunched over a pad, sketching furiously. The wind teased her blond hair. She was beautiful.

"May I see your drawings?"

She sketched with charcoal, not looking up. "Are you sure you want to look? There are ones of you in here."

"Did you draw me as a gargoyle? Or a cyclops?" he asked, lounging back in a deck chair and propping his foot on the bolted down table between the seating.

She glanced up. "Why would I do that?"

"Since we talked about our past arguments."

Fish plopped in the brief silence before she answered, "You've been nothing but understanding and patient with me, with this whole situation. No matter what else happens, I won't forget that."

"Whatever else happens?" Trepidation kinked the muscles in his neck.

"If you get tired of having an amnesiac wife."

"I could never get tired of you."

Her cheeks flushed pink as she glanced at him through her eyelashes. His mind swirled, thinking of last night. Of her body pressed against his and the scent of her coconut shampoo. And how he'd wanted so much more than to just sleep next to her.

How he still wanted that.

She seemed to read his thoughts, her blush fading. Awareness flitted across her face. An expression that almost looked like longing.

The sound of another fish jumping out of the water brought them back to reality. He shook his head.

She passed over the pad of drawings. "Here. Feel free to look."

She tucked her hair behind her ear and chewed her nail as he flipped through the book.

There were pages upon pages of sketches. Some scenes of the beach house. Some of boats in the harbor. Thomas in a Santa hat.

All so damn good, the details grabbing his heart. "You've been busy."

"I feel like there are thoughts needing to pour out. I don't have to think or talk, just... Oh, I don't know how to describe it other than to say it's like meditation."

He flipped to the next page. Half-finished drawings of him sleeping. She seemed to fixate on his face. Mostly his eyes. As if she was trying to figure out something about him. Her sketches were beautiful. Hyperrealistic. He'd forgotten how talented she was with charcoal and pencils.

The last sketch in the book sucked the air from his chest. It was a montage of images. Items of their joint past. Did she remember?

It was a scene of a room. On the desk, there was a globe with a cracked stand. A Moroccan rug on the ground. All souvenirs—all representing moments in their life together. If she didn't know what these were, what did the drawings mean? Why had she stumbled onto these particular items? He couldn't decide whether to tell her or not. What would be helpful?

Truth. As much as he could give her.

"There are items here that you received over those missing years, gifts I gave you."

She gasped. "Like what?"

"The rug right here." He pointed to the sketch, careful not to smudge the material, "It was the first gift I ever gave you. When you were living in that tiny apartment with the tile in your bedroom. You said you hated how cold your feet were in the mornings. Even then, I knew you liked those rich colors. Items with a bit of history. I picked it up on a business trip."

She considered his words, staring hard at the sketch. "I woke up with this scene in my head. I thought it was from a dream…but maybe my memories are trying to come back after all."

"It's quite possible."

"What else is from our past?"

"The globe with the cracked stand."

"That's a strange gift. Where's it from?" She crinkled her nose and adjusted her sunglasses again.

"Well it didn't start out cracked. It cracked in our move. But I got it for our one-year anniversary. It was a blank globe. Ceramic. You painted it. It's got quotes over where the countries ought to be. Quotes about art and life. I've always thought you should replicate it and sell them."

She smiled at him. "Do you think the art supplies gift made me think of that?"

"Could be."

"What about being on the yacht? What will that help me remember?"

"Honestly? Arguing. You were angry with me for buying this. You thought the money could have been better spent. But then we fought about pretty much everything then."

"I appreciate you being honest."

"I want you to trust me. You believe that, right?"

"I do. I'm just not sure you want me to remember everything. You seem very into this fresh start. All the control is on your side since you have the pieces of the past and I only get what other people tell me."

He couldn't deny the truth in that. He owed her more, better. Hell, he owed her the unvarnished truth, but couldn't bring himself to go quite that far when they were so close to having everything they'd wanted. Time on the yacht offered them a window of time away from the world and he needed to embrace that fully.

"Alaina, I have an idea. Let's use this time to pretend we're two different people. Strangers who've met and are stuck on this ostentatious yacht together. Strangers attracted to each other and ready to get to know each other." He loosened the cap on the water bottle and handed it to her.

His gaze met hers, and he could swear the air crackled with the static of a lightning strike even though there wasn't a cloud in the sky.

She grabbed it and flashed him a grin. "I'm game."

* * *

Vibrant pinks of the sunset blurred into deeper purples. The heat of the day was behind them, the cool ocean breeze nudging Alaina's skin toward goose bumps. She ran a hand over her exposed leg, hoping to generate some warmth.

Embers of sunlight caused the yacht to glow. While she was conscious of how expensive this outing was, she had to admit there was some charm to it all. The lulling rock of the yacht in the water. The heavy smell of salt in the air. Relaxing. Intimate. It was easy to feel as if they were the only two people in the whole world with the captain and crew dismissed for a few hours and other boats so far away.

And in some ways, that'd been a good thing.

But she still couldn't help feeling slightly uneasy. He hadn't denied wanting this fresh start, or taking the power it gave him. Even when she agreed to get to know him anew, she wondered what he really thought of her. Of all of this.

"You look chilled." Porter pushed his deck chair closer to hers. He had a thick blanket in his hand. It was covered in a sprawling cursive print. She squinted in the dying light to see what it said. Looked like lines from a novel. Was that a purchase she'd made?

"I've definitely been warmer. That's for sure." Although there was heat building inside her just from looking at him, having him near. Their night sleeping together had brought a new level of intimacy to their relationship. One that made her yearn to take that to the next level.

"Luckily for you, I come prepared." He draped the blanket across her shoulders, his hands brushing her shoulders and sending another shiver through her.

Definitely the electric sort of shiver born of heat not cold.

She pulled the blanket tight, closing it around her body against the ache for contact with him. Did he want this as much as she did? What would happen afterward?

"So generous," she teased him, but she was grateful for his attentiveness. Even her nose was cold.

"I don't know about that. There is a catch, you

see." The sunset glinted in his eyes. His beard-stubbled face was serious.

"Oh?"

"It's going to cost you a date, lady. And you're going to have to share that blanket." A mischievous twinkle danced in his dark eyes, reaching his lips.

Butterflies filled her stomach, and her breasts tingled with increasing need. His relaxed smile sparked a fierce need for him; the new ease of being with him stirred her.

Deeply.

He was asking for more than a shared night in a bed and she could sense they both knew that.

Clenching the blanket tighter in her fists, she returned his gaze steadily. "I don't know about that. That's a pretty tall demand."

Feeling bold and ready to take a risk that she prayed would pay off, she held out a side of the blanket for him to sit next to her. He filled the gaping space in an instant with his big, warm presence.

"How 'bout a game?" he asked, gathering her closer, his hard thigh against her legs.

"I like games." She liked *him*. A lot.

"Thought you might. I'll ask a question. And you have to answer it. And then you can do the same to me." He pivoted his body to face her.

She nodded, her hair snagging on his five o'clock shadow. "I like it. But I'm going first. Worst drink you've ever had?"

"Worst drink? Hmm. In college, a friend dared me to drink a bar mat—which is basically a mix of all the alcohol that spills during the night as a shot. I never made that mistake again." He shuddered at the memory.

"That is absolutely disgusting." She laughed, unable to imagine him losing control in any way. "What in the world made you go along with that?"

"Now, now, Alaina." He nudged her shoulder gently. "You only get one question at a time. It's my turn. If you had to be stuck in one television show for the rest of your life, which one would it be?"

Now that was a hard one. "Well. And you keep in mind I'm working with outdated information. But I'd have to say I'd like to be stuck in *Scooby-Doo*. The original series. I could totally drive around in the Mystery Machine. I half wanted to be a detective when I was younger because of that show. Definitely my favorite growing up."

"*Scooby-Doo?* I would never have guessed that one. You'd have the brains of Velma and the beauty of Daphne. You would've been the powerhouse." He put his arm around her back, drawing her closer to him as he leaned them down to look at the first evening stars.

She turned to half lie on his chest, her ear pressed against the steady thud of his heart. "Ha-ha. Absolute favorite meal? Like the kind you could eat again and again and never get sick of?"

He exhaled deeply. "You do know how to ask the tough questions. I would eat Dunkaroos for every meal. I love the frosting."

"Porter...really? Out of all the food in the

world…Dunkaroos?" She lifted her head off his chest to stare at his face. Smile lines pushed at his cheeks as he attempted to look completely serious.

"Oh, yeah. Completely." She arched her brow at him. But the smile stuck to her face, anyway.

"My turn again. Let's see—who was your first kiss?"

"Oh, lord. I haven't thought about Bobby Dagana in ages. I was fourteen. He walked me home and kissed me on my doorstep. But my mom saw the whole thing happen and teased me for the rest of the day."

"If I had known you when we were younger, I would have kissed you before Bobby Dagana had ever thought about it." He massaged the back of her head. Fingers tracing circles in her scalp.

"Mmm. That feels nice. Could you keep doing that while I think of another question?" She held on to his side, hooked her fingers in his belt loop. She could have sworn the vessel rocked under her feet even as she knew that would be virtually undetectable on the large luxury yacht.

"Nope. Sorry. That's your question…I'm kidding." He captured a lock of her hair and wrapped it around his finger.

"What are you thinking about right now?" Her heart was in her throat as she waited for the answer. The seconds felt like mini eternities.

"Honestly? You. How beautiful you are. How lucky I am." He said it without a trace of sarcasm or humor. He squeezed her arm. Silence fell between them.

She swallowed hard. "Really lucky to have your life turned upside down because I can't remember even meeting you?"

Her eyes stung with tears.

"Ah, Alaina," he sighed, stroking her face. "I don't deserve you."

"Why do you say that?"

"Because you came out here with me today, even though you seemed to have sensed the yacht wasn't neutral territory for us. Why *did* you come out on the yacht with me?"

* * *

Where the hell had that come from?

Porter wanted to kick himself. He'd been five seconds away from romancing his wife back into his bed again. Then he'd sabotaged it by asking a question to stop their progress in its tracks.

"The yacht seems to have been a bone of contention between us and I wanted to try to heal that."

"Did you remember something about it?" He felt as if his marriage was one big ticking time bomb, set to explode the second she regained her full memory. He had to make the most of their time together before that happened.

"It's more like a sensation, feelings." She tapped her temple, her forehead furrowed. "Intuition, I guess. But no, I don't remember."

A reprieve. For now.

He searched for the right words to strike a balance between honesty and gaining her trust without spilling all. "We did argue, pretty heatedly. You thought it was a waste of money, that we didn't need it, wouldn't be using it often enough to warrant the expense."

"It is a nice boat." She drew a lazy circle on his chest with her finger.

He struggled to focus.

"Boat? That's something you ski behind or paddle."

"Ah, so the big boat is important to you." She patted his chest. "That's rather Freudian."

He didn't take the bait and argue with her as he would have in the past. Instead, he worked to explain his feelings rather than offer up a knee-jerk reaction. Over the past few weeks, he'd pushed aside her feelings for his own, and he knew if he wanted his family to stay intact, he needed to try a different strategy.

"The escape is important to me. There's no office here. It's the anticonstruction site, no land."

"Oh." She blinked fast, her hands falling to her lap. "Did you tell me that before?"

"I didn't," he admitted. "I should have."

She stayed silent so long he wondered if she would change the subject altogether.

Then she looked up at him, her blue eyes searching his face. "Would I have heard you?"

He hadn't expected that from her. Maybe they were both changing, making something good happen from the hell of the car accident that had stolen her memory.

"Maybe. Maybe not. I honestly can't answer that, Alaina. And you've mentioned before that it's not fair I'm the filter for all your memories and questions." He reached forward and slid a disc holder off the table. "We're tied to this house for now. But I compiled all the videos and photos of our Tallahassee home. When we get back, if you're ready and want to, I will try my best to help you connect with people who knew both of us."

"Thank you. Truly. This means more to me than…well, more than any expensive gift." She took the disc from him and held it to her chest. "This is what I'm talking about. You're really trying to hear what I need, to help us trust each other. I can feel that."

Trust. Now that was a sticky word. But the

doctor had warned against pushing her too fast. Maybe that was a convenient excuse now for not being more open, but damn, she felt good in his arms. He didn't want to say anything to make her pull away.

She set the disc aside and rested her palms on his chest, the invitation clear in her gaze. "And I want to be closer to you, even if it's just on a physical level."

They'd been married a long time. He recognized the authenticity of the desire in her eyes, the passion in her husky voice. Some things between them didn't need words or memories. Their bodies recognized each other.

Still, he had to ask, to keep what fragile trust they'd built.

"Alaina," he said, taking her face in his hands, "are you sure this is what you want?"

"Absolutely certain," she whispered against his mouth an instant before she kissed him.

In a flash of insight, as he wrapped his arms around her, he realized why he'd asked about the boat. To deflect her from pressing for more on why he felt he wasn't a good husband. He was changing, learning from his mistakes, but he still wasn't ready to admit he hadn't been up-front about how close they'd been to divorce before the accident. He wanted to make his family whole before they dealt with that truth.

He was a jerk.

And the worst part? He still couldn't bring himself to back away from this chance to have Alaina again.

Every step of the way to their cabin below, she kissed him. Deeply. Urgently.

Hungrily.

Alaina savored the taste of Porter on her tongue. The sensations pulsing through her were new and familiar all at once. Surreal. Sensual.

The touch of his hand, the rasp of his beard-stubbled face, the scent of him—all of it turned her inside out. Nothing in her life made sense. Her past was a jumble. Her present a strange haze.

But she was certain of this. Of needing Porter.

Of their undeniable chemistry. Of the evening that had sparked her back to life in a way she was somehow certain she'd never felt before.

Her feet tangled with his as they moved through the corridor, sconces lighting the way toward the main cabin. He met her kiss for kiss, snaking his hands into the mess of her wavy hair. His steps slowing, he pressed her against the wall to deepen the contact. Pressed her closer to him. Her back against the polished cypress wainscoting.

And then he broke the kiss to stare at her. His coal-dark eyes searched her face, looking for an answer to his unasked question. And she knew. He was wrestling with this step and the fact that she didn't recall their marriage.

But she recalled their now. She felt the connection. She didn't believe in love at first sight, but there was a sense of their history still binding them, curling through some part of her mind.

So she leaned in for another kiss and reassured him.

"I want this." She breathed against his mouth.

Then nipped his lower lip. She let her hand travel to the tender flesh between his shirt and pant line.

His head fell back with a growl of desire. Need fueled the air between them. He lifted her legs to wrap around his waist. She hooked her heels behind him, her core pressed to his, her arms looped around his neck. Her body was on fire for him.

Porter.

Her husband.

He carried her the rest of the way down the hall, past framed photos of Florida island scenery and fishing expeditions. And she had to admit, this yacht had a romantic appeal. She appreciated the sense of escape, being away from the world, just the two of them floating alone in the world.

Porter shouldered open the door to their master bedroom, and then shouldered the door closed after him. The lighting was dimmer here, but she didn't care much about the surroundings anymore. Only the man touching her.

And that big bed waiting for them.

Gently, he eased her back onto the soft comforter carefully, stretching out on top of her. He propped himself on his forearms, but there was no missing the rigid length of him pressing against her belly.

A smile spread across her lips as she met his gaze. In his face, she saw his desire matched hers. Frenzy. Fire. Longing.

"Alaina. I've missed you. So damned much." He punctuated each word with a kiss before angling back up onto an elbow, putting enough space between them to pluck at their clothes.

One, then the other, he peeled off her layered shirts and bared her lacy bra to the moonlight and low flickering sconces. Reverently, he ran gentle fingers across the peaks of her breasts. Her nipples tightened in response. Anticipation lit beneath her skin and she reached for him, needed to feel his bare flesh against hers. She skimmed off his shirt and unzipped his jeans with impatience, her hands brushing his as he peeled away her leggings.

Finally, finally, they were both naked. The heat of his skin seared her and she wondered how she could have ever forgotten this man.

Porter lowered himself on top of her. Skimmed her collarbone with kisses. Traveled with soft lips back to her mouth. He held one of her hands above her head as he skimmed off her underwear.

She arched her body toward him. Slick with need for him. His fingers teasing her, taking her desire to another level.

His breath was against her skin again. Kissing her hip, hands sketching along her breasts, then his mouth there as well, licking and drawing her in until she bit back a cry of ecstasy.

She pushed herself up, meeting Porter's eyes as she reached for the hard length of him. His jaw flexed, eyes fluttering as she stroked him. His lips found hers again. Needing the contact.

Hooking her legs around his waist again, she pulled him closer. Pulled him into her, the thick press of him filling her. They were anchored together. Joined by something more than the physical.

There was a deliberate rhythm to their coupling. The frenzy shifting into something even more intimate. Something that didn't rely on the past, that only existed between the people they were now. A throaty moan rolled through her. Made her dizzy as he stroked her. She writhed, hands twisting in the blanket.

Each deep thrust sent her closer to a wave of ecstasy about to crest. They pushed farther up the deck chair until she was pressed up against the edge. Their bodies moved as one in a familiar rhythm.

He kissed her deeply on her mouth. Her neck. She practically melted into him as he brought her to the cusp of release, slowed, held back, then thrust deeper to drive her the rest of the way into completion.

She wrapped her legs tighter around him, her heels digging into his ass. She kissed him, fiercely, deeply, taking his hoarse shout of completion into her mouth, aftershocks rippling through her again and again.

Their first time together.

Or rather her first time with him.

That thought threatened to steal the bliss still shimmering through her.

As she held him, their bodies slick with sweat, she knew. They'd done this before. She knew him, not in a concrete memory, but in an elusive feeling she wanted to grasp and hold on to but couldn't quite reach.

However she knew, this man was her husband.

Nine

Peace settled inside him like a whisper, like the breeze coming in off the ocean. Alaina had pulled on his polo shirt to keep out the night chill. It looked right on her. She pressed herself against him, head resting on his shoulder. Her soft arms draped over his bare chest. The downy blanket closed them in together, cocooning them in that peace.

Except with that peace came the reminder that he still hadn't told her everything about the state of their marriage before the accident. They'd moved to another level here and he couldn't keep hiding the facts from her for much longer under the excuse of protecting her or rebuilding their family.

She had always been a strong, independent woman. That hadn't changed. He could feel the restlessness in her to regain her life. He owed it to her to do everything he could to help. And he would. He resolved to give her—them—the foundation, the memory, of a beautiful Christmas together, and then just before New Year's he could tell her everything he could about their past. Hopefully she, too, would see that the New Year offered a new beginning, symbolically and literally.

At first, keeping Alaina had been about reestablishing their family at all costs, but as he learned new things about her and realized the mistakes he'd made that had contributed to their discord, he knew he didn't just want the family. He wanted her. He wanted them. Together. In love.

He'd do anything to keep her with him like this. He hadn't realized how broken they'd been before. But tonight—tonight they'd connected as they had when they were just falling in love.

A new conviction overtook him. Porter wanted to help ease her memories back. He was not afraid of her leaving. Of her wanting a life without him. They fit. They were a team.

A family.

"What was our first time together like?" Alaina's voice carried on the wind.

Porter took a deep breath. "Are you sure you wouldn't rather remember that on your own and not have my words tangled up in those memories?"

She looked up her chest at him, her blue eyes still hazy with passion. "I want to hear how you remember us."

"Okay, then." His hand settled on the soft curve of her hip. "I'll do my best to set the stage for you. I came to your apartment for dinner. You swore you could make the best steak and stuffed mushrooms. I brought a bottle of wine. You were in a bright green dress. Red lipstick. Your hair was curled. We ate. And you were right." Paused to kiss her. He never wanted to stop kissing her.

He whispered in her ear, "Best steak and stuffed mushrooms ever. And then." He nipped down her neck again, tasting the mix of sea salt and sweat. "The rest is history."

A breathy sigh escaped her lips a second before she angled to press her mouth to his. "Let's make history again."

He growled his approval.

Her hands slid around his waist and shifted on his lap. He spanned her waist and brought her closer. She wriggled against his erection, sending a fresh jolt of desire through him. The scent of her shampoo, the salty air and their lovemaking combined into a heady aphrodisiac.

The blanket, in addition to the dark, gave them an air of privacy. And even though all the boats were too far away for anyone to see them, there was also a sexiness to being out in the open this way with her, under the stars. Sex between them had always been good, even with the stress of the fertility treatments, but there was a freedom between them now.

A new connection tonight.

Her hands skimmed across his bare chest, her head falling back to expose the curve of her neck, encouraging him wordlessly. He didn't need more of an invitation to make the most of this chance to be with her again.

He slipped his hands under the shirt—his shirt on her, the cotton warm from her body. Her silky smooth skin called to him, enticed him to explore further. He skimmed up to cup her breasts, circling his thumbs over her nipples as he kissed the curve of her neck. Her low moan of excitement encouraged him to continue. He stroked down her side, tucking his fingers into her panties, the string along her hip a fragile barrier that gave way with a twist and snap.

Humming her approval, she made fast work of unzipping his jeans. He swept away her underwear, the scrap of satin almost as soft as her skin. The moist heat of her pressed against him. He'd never wanted her—or anyone—more than at this moment. She was everything, his every fantasy come to life. She was…Alaina.

Resting her hands on his shoulders, she raised up, then lowered herself onto him, taking him inside her. Exactly where he wanted to be for as long as possible. A challenge with her hips rolling against him in an arousing wriggle.

He cupped her bottom and brought her closer still, thrusting up as she threaded her fingers through his hair, tugging slightly. Her husky sighs drove him crazy with wanting her, drove all thoughts of their past away until only the present mattered.

And hell yeah, he knew he was making excuses to be with her even with secrets between them. But right then, he didn't care.

The wind blew her hair forward and around his face, as if binding them more closely. The silky strands teased his senses. Everything about her was sensual. Her hair, yes, even her hair turned him on, drove him closer to the edge until he bit back the urge to come, waiting for her. Touching her and stroking her until her breath hitched in that way he knew meant she was close, so close. And then her orgasm massaged him over the edge to his own release. Their groans tangled up, tossed around in the wind like her hair.

Each ripple of his release rolled through him like waves along the water, one after the other. Elemental. So damn perfect, all the more so because she sighed her bliss against his neck.

Cradling her to him, he reclined back onto the deck, holding her, the blanket still secured around them. He drew in ragged breaths of ocean air, his heart hammering in his chest.

Alaina sagged back until they lay side by side with a deep exhale. "Porter, it's not fair that you know exactly what I want and I know so little about what turns you on."

"So little?" He laughed. "Trust me—your instincts are spot-on."

"Hmmm… Maybe I'm remembering things on a subconscious level."

Her words chilled him into silence for an instant before he said, "Like what?"

"Nothing specific really." She linked hands with him. "Just impressions. A sense of knowing you."

He squeezed her hand. "I like the sound of that. We're still married underneath everything that's happened."

She just made that *hmmm* noise again and let the silence settle.

He rolled onto his side, propping his head on his hand. "Should we turn in?"

She traced his bottom lip. "I want to sleep here with you on the boat, but I can't leave Thomas overnight. Even knowing he's just there on shore—"

Porter kissed her fingertips. Drew her close. "I understand and I agree. Let's go see our son."

He wanted their focus to be on their family, their future, and Thomas was an important part of what would bind them together even after she regained her memories. If Porter could give Alaina the perfect family Christmas, she would understand why he wanted their family to remain intact, why he'd waited to tell her the truth about their tumultuous past. She'd understand, and she'd forgive him so they could create a happy, stable family environment for their son.

Or at least he thought she would forgive him. The trouble with Alaina's amnesia, however, was that she wasn't the same woman he'd once known.

The moon glow washed the beach in a pale silver light, softening the edges of their mansion like a watercolor image. Alaina took it in, seeing a beauty in the place she'd missed before. This might not be her personal pick of a home, but there was a blessing in having access to this kind of magnificent landscape and a peaceful escape where she could recover.

She curled in a tight ball, hugging her knees, wrapped in a blanket on the hammock. The light breeze rocked her back and forth, keeping time with the crash of the waves.

She'd come out here after they'd checked on Thomas while Porter went to scavenge for food. She'd brought a laptop with her to watch the disc he'd made, filled with images of their home. Such a thoughtful gesture.

And the more she glanced at the photographs of her life, the more she was excited for the return trip to Tallahassee. For life with Porter and Thomas. For her shot at having a family.

She looked up from the laptop, glancing at the house next door, Sage's home. Could the woman's comment about another man visiting be trusted? Was there a hidden agenda in her statement?

Or could there have been another man? Alaina didn't feel as if she ever could have been the sort to cheat on her husband but what did she really know about their marriage?

A burn started along her skin as she thought of her stalker ex-boyfriend from long ago. Could he have been lurking around again after so many years? Porter hadn't mentioned him, but perhaps she should bring up the subject of Douglas and simply ask that they look into his whereabouts.

An outline of an approaching figure took

shape out of the misty night. Her eyes adjusted from the glare of the laptop to the darkness of the moonlit beach and she recognized her husband. Sagging with relief, she closed her laptop and set it aside to focus on this renewed connection with Porter. He strode down the bluff, sure-footed, a pizza in one hand, baby monitor in the other.

His smile widened as he placed the box on the Adirondack chair and sat next to her on the hammock.

"You're the only woman I ever met who would rather be romanced with deep-dish pizza than the offer of lobster." Porter passed her a slice.

Steam oozed off the cheese—the scent of tomatoes, garlic and oregano dancing around her. She blew cool air on her slice, eager to dive in. "The videos you put together of the Tallahassee house were very thoughtful. I haven't gotten to watch them all, but I took a quick peek and I like the house."

"I'm glad. We'll be celebrating New Year's there with our son."

"And your mom?"

"She won't be with us. I'm still not sure why she's here." Even in the muted light, she could see his eyes darken at the mention of his mother. His mouth went tight.

In the deepest part of her core, Alaina wanted to set her family right. Her whole family, which included Courtney, too.

"She loves you. She wants to see your child." She set the plate of pizza down and ran a comforting hand down his back.

"Our child. You're a good mother, Alaina." He kissed her forehead.

"Thank you. These definitely aren't the easiest of circumstances to become a first-time parent." She looked down at her slice of pizza. "Your mother said I used to volunteer in the NICU, back when we were trying to conceive."

"You did. You were so generous and brave to do that. Like I said, you're a born mother."

She'd tried to envision herself in the hospital holding babies. Had volunteering helped ease the ache inside her over not being able to become pregnant? Or had it deepened her sense of loss?

"Your mother and I may be different, but that doesn't mean she loves you any less than I love Thomas."

"Like I said, you're generous. She wasn't very nice to you when we got married."

"Why was that?" She'd gathered that much. Pieced it together from her conversations with her mother-in-law. But Alaina wondered if that even mattered now. The introduction of their child reminded Alaina that there was more at stake in this family than petty fights.

"I was never really sure and you didn't bad-mouth her so I never found out."

Alaina nodded, wondering if the animosity had just been a misunderstanding. And realizing that her mother-in-law had never intentionally sabotaged them. She'd kept her reservations about Alaina to herself. And there was something to be said for that. "She must not have bad-mouthed me, either, or you would know what the problem was."

"I hadn't thought about that."

"I just think it is something to consider. And besides, your mom and I are fine now. We have a fresh start. And she wants to be a part of the family—a part of our lives. Part of Thomas's life. I can feel it." A gust of wind pushed the ends of her hair into her eyes. She removed a ponytail holder from her wrist and piled her hair on top of her head in a messy bun.

"Oh, yeah. She wants to be part of the family. But only when it suits her." Bitterness dripped from his words. He ran a hand through his hair, exhaling deeply.

She picked up his hand in hers and twined their fingers together. "So…what should we get your mom for Christmas? And should we think of a neutral gift for her tax-attorney boyfriend? You know, just in case he is here. I'd hate for him to have nothing to open up if he spends Christmas with us."

Porter's jaw tightened and he dropped her hand. "I'm cold, aren't you?"

"Not terribly. Not with you and this blanket."

She tried to catch his eye. To get him to stay and talk to her. To calm down and let her in. They could work through this together if he would only open up.

Was this something that used to happen in the past? Were these the kinds of arguments they'd had before?

"I think it's time to go inside. We have a big day tomorrow. Lots of wrapping to do. We don't want to get sick." He started to gather the remains of the pizza and dishes. He kissed her forehead again, then he started for the beach house, retreating into the dark space between the beach and the mansion.

Leaving her with a cold feeling in her stomach no blanket could insulate.

Of all the times for his temper to explode, this was probably the worst one imaginable.

Porter had sought sanctuary in his office. Tried to lose himself in work. To cool down. To figure out why he had got so angry with Alaina.

He knew he'd been unreasonable. And he was

afraid he'd blown his second chance with her. Maybe she'd see he wasn't worthy of her love and time. Maybe this would be the trigger that brought all of her memories rushing back. But not the good memories. The dark ones. All of their fights.

Without even realizing it, he'd bumped over from his spreadsheet and projections charts to the internet. He'd begun to scour his normal stockpile of online shopping websites. Looking for a gift for his mother. Alaina was right. He needed to figure something out.

And not just a gift for his mom. Also how to fix the space he'd placed between him and his wife. Again. Had he been too selfish keeping their past a secret? Put Alaina at too much of a disadvantage by not sharing the darker parts of their marriage?

A knock pulled his attention to the door, and damn, how ironic, there his mother stood.

"Good evening, Porter. I was just thinking about what I should get Thomas for Christmas. Now, I know you and Alaina just finished your big shopping trip, but I thought we'd compare lists."

Now his mother was ready to play Santa? After all these years of virtually ignoring the holidays? Not that he begrudged his son the presents by any means, but he also didn't want Thomas to expect something from Courtney only to have her go back to her old ways later. Porter pursed his lips. Felt them turn white with tension.

"Clothes would be fine." It came out like a bark. "Or set away money for his college education. Whatever you want."

Courtney nodded, straightening her green silk scarf as she stepped deeper into the room. "This place reminds me so much of that Christmas we spent in the Keys when you were younger. Do you remember?"

"I do. But I think the beach house is closer to the house you rented the Christmas we went to Virginia Beach."

"Sometimes the places run together for me. I

never liked to repeat holiday locations. Too depressing." A sad sort of smile set on her mouth.

Old habits died hard. When was the last time he and Alaina had spent a holiday in Tallahassee? He could have brought them home. To start their lives together in the space they'd cocreated. But instead, he'd fled and brought them here. Maybe there were some similarities between him and his mother after all.

"So are you serious about this guy?" Porter asked, shutting down his computer for the night.

Courtney shook her head. "No. I'm done with the search for my forever love. After your father left me…well, I'm not sure I've ever been the same. I loved him. I really did. But then he left and I was pregnant…" Her voice trailed off. She stared at her son with shining eyes.

"Mom…I'm sorry." A pang ricocheted through his heart. He'd had no idea she'd ever felt that way about anyone.

"Oh, honey. Don't look at me like that. I know things haven't been perfect for us. But I'm so glad that this was the path of my life. It gave you to me, and I've never once regretted it," she said, wrapping him in a hug.

It wasn't a particularly tight hug, but it wasn't one of those air hugs that she normally gave. From his mom, this was a lot.

He'd been so focused on his experience of childhood, on what she'd lacked as a mother, that he'd failed to see she was every bit as damaged as he was by the guy who'd bailed on them.

Never before had he considered what his father had done to his mother. Never had he thought about how betrayed and lonely his mother must have felt.

He was a selfish bastard for missing that.

"Thanks, Mom. I'm glad you're in Thomas's life." He hugged her back before stepping away.

Just as Alaina's scream echoed from above.

Ten

Alaina shot upright on the bed where she'd fallen asleep on top of the covers. The nightmare filled her brain like toxic fumes. Except it wasn't a dream. It was a memory, but from five years ago. One she hadn't forgotten but had instead pushed back because it was too painful to remember on a daily basis.

Why was she dreaming of an ex-boyfriend now? Of that hellish last time she'd seen Douglas? Of what he'd done to her?

Porter charged through the door, looked around the room as if searching for an intruder, then rushed to their bedroom, his face filled with concern—and fear. "Alaina, what's wrong? Are you okay?"

Thomas started shrieking in the next room, his plaintive cries cutting through the fog in her mind. She slid her feet off the bed. "I need to go to him—"

Courtney called from the open doorway, apparently having followed her son upstairs, "I'll take care of the baby. You two…talk. I promise not to drop him," she said in a halfhearted joke that fell a little flat. Then she left, heels clicking double time down the hall.

Heart still racing, Alaina waited until her son's cries quieted at Courtney's cooing and only then did she sag back against the headboard. Porter crossed to close the door, then returned to her, sitting on the edge of the bed while she tried to catch her breath. Returning to the present was tough. The night terror's claws were still buried deep in her.

Porter stroked her tangled hair back from her face. "What's going on?"

"I had another nightmare about Douglas." It

seemed a pale word for what she'd experienced. Especially since the event had really happened to her five years ago.

She shivered at the thought. Intellectually, she knew it was long ago, but it felt so much closer to the present because of the amnesia. The chill settled deep in her gut and she tugged the down comforter tighter around her even though it made no sense that she would be so cold.

"How was this dream different from the other one about him?"

"This time, he didn't just stalk me, or slap me. Douglas hurt me…more. So much more."

He went still. Very still. "More?"

"You know what I mean." She made a vague gesture with her hands, as if they could speak what she hated to verbalize.

"I'm not sure I do."

"You must know." She looked up at him sharply. "We were married for almost four years. You have to know what he did to me." A desperate, fearful note entered her voice as she searched his face. Hoping the answers were there.

It was bad enough she had to relive it in her dreams. She didn't want to. So many times she'd resented that Porter needed to fill in the blanks in her memory. But she didn't want to recall one second more of this than she already did.

His eyes narrowed. "You told me how he verbally abused you. Your fights escalated and he hit you. You left him because of that, then he stalked you. Completely unacceptable, and you told him it had to stop." He grabbed for her hand gently.

A simple touch, but it gave her the courage she'd been lacking.

A courage that was all the more necessary as she realized she might have omitted a very big facet of her past from him. Why would she have done that?

"I honestly never explained to you what happened after I left him?" she pressed. "Why I got the restraining order?"

"I assumed you spoke with the police right away." He frowned. For an odd moment their roles were reversed as she had answers that he didn't know about.

She couldn't say she liked the feeling on this side of the fence, either. "I did speak to the police, then and later. And you really don't know this? You never did a background check on me?"

"I'm insulted you would think that of me."

"You seem like the kind of guy who would learn as much as you could about an important person in your life."

"I seem like a control freak, you mean?" A laugh escaped his lips, an effort to put her at ease she realized.

"No, um, you just seem assertive." She searched for the right words but her nerves were so damn frayed. "Detail oriented."

"Well, that's diplomatic."

She dropped her gaze, cheeks burning at the memory. The reality catching in her throat. "You're not like Douglas at all." She understood that absolutely. "But I think maybe since I woke up from the coma I've been fearing that you're like him. That the amnesia upsets the balance of control between us, and on some level that's been frightening to me."

"I'm not sure I'm following what you're trying to tell me." He pinched the bridge of his nose. "What happened that gave you nightmares? Did you remember the time he showed up here?"

She looked up sharply. "He came *here*?"

"Once, yes, he did. You freaked out. I arrived home just in time, and…" He clenched his hands in fists. "I hit him and the police were called. He did a little time in jail for violating the restraining order and that was that. We never saw him again. Last I heard he got arrested for assault and is back in prison."

That must have been what Sage saw. There wasn't some other man she'd been seeing during her marital troubles. There hadn't been cheating in the marriage because no way in hell would she have ever, ever slept with Douglas again. And thank God, he was out of her life, unable to reach her.

Relief melted through her, dulling the edges

of her fear enough that she could say the words out loud to Porter.

Her husband, a man who'd been there for her, who supported her as an equal. She might not have shared the full truth before, but she needed to share it now.

"Douglas did more than hit me once before we split up. When he started stalking me, I thought he would lose interest in time but it got worse." Even thinking about it, just remembering those months brought back the old terror, and then the pain.

Porter rubbed a hand along her back in soothing circles, staying silent but present, waiting.

"One night, after work, he was lurking around my apartment. I don't know how many times he'd done it before. He said he'd been watching me, studying my habits. And the time had come for us to be together again."

A breath hissed between Porter's teeth.

"Usually I had someone walk me to my car, but not that night. So yes, he'd probably been waiting every night and stayed away those other times because he was such a coward. He would have never dared come after me if I had a protector."

"Please don't say you're blaming yourself for whatever happened. You have to know you didn't deserve the hell and the betrayal that bastard brought into your life."

"No, I don't blame myself. I understand he would have found me alone sometime. It's impossible to stay on guard 24/7. He preyed on me because my family was dead and I had very few connections to check up on me." She said the words by rote, knowing them to be true, but still wondering what else she could have done. Maybe she should have moved across the country. "It's not unreasonable to expect to live my life."

His throat moved in a hard swallow. "Do you want to tell me what happened?"

She covered his hand quickly, realizing she should have told him right away. "He didn't rape me, if that's what you're thinking."

"I'm not thinking anything. I'm waiting for you to tell me."

She exhaled hard. "He beat the hell out of me in the parking lot. Completely. He hit me and kicked me, damn near killed me before he walked away as if we'd just had a disagreement over what cereal to have for breakfast. I crawled into the car and tried to drive myself to the hospital."

"Why wasn't he locked away for good, then?"

Alaina picked at an imaginary piece of lint. The memory swelled before her again, rising up in the depths of her stomach. She took a steadying breath. She needed more air in her lungs. "Family connections and a good lawyer were able to convince a jury my injuries resulted from driving into a ditch as I tried to take myself to the hospital."

"The auto accident that made it difficult for you to conceive." A flicker of understanding passed over his face.

"Yes. Except it wasn't an accident. And the jury didn't believe it, in spite of the restraining order. His lawyers said I was unbalanced and trying to set him up. They convinced the jury."

"That's such bull," he blurted out.

"I agree."

She'd felt so helpless and alone without even someone to sit by her side in court. She'd isolated herself from everyone but her work friends by then, not wanting Douglas to lash out at someone close to her. It was the double cruelty of domestic abuse—an abuser isolated a woman and then, scared and mortified, a woman isolated herself more.

"What happened?" he asked.

"In the end they settled on a restraining order against both of us." She stared at her hands. "And you truly didn't know this? I never told you?"

"You didn't." He shook his head, and then, looking at her, his shoulders tensed. "I hope you believe me."

"I do believe you, actually. But that makes me wonder why I didn't share this before now, though." Had she clung to some kind of old sense of shame? Or simply hoped for a new start? "It's strange, especially since that played a part in our inability to have kids—you said it was both of us, though."

"It was. The scar tissue around your fallopian tubes and my low sperm count worked against each other." He took her hands in his. "But that's all a moot point. I am so sorry for what you went through."

"You're not angry with me for not telling you?"

"I'm…frustrated. I wish I'd known. I wish you'd trusted me enough to tell me."

She wanted to ask him what was wrong between them that she wouldn't share something so important, but maybe he was puzzling through that even now. What was wrong with her? Why hadn't she trusted him? That question scared her most of all because in spite of her concerns since coming home from the hospital, she'd grown closer to him over the past couple of weeks. She could see them building a life together with their child.

But that nightmare was a threat to her future. She could feel it. A simmering unease filled her, rooted in the fact that she hadn't trusted him with such fundamental knowledge about her as a person. She hadn't confided her deepest fears to him and she didn't like what that revealed about their relationship. Or at least, their old relationship.

Was it foolish of her to hope they had started to build something stronger than what they'd had? Something that could really last? More than anything, she wanted to keep the connection they'd found. Especially when she felt so completely adrift in the world.

She needed Porter. Needed to reclaim that connection to him on an elemental level.

The last thing Porter expected right now was for Alaina to push him back onto the bed and straddle his lap. No doubting her intent, though. She planned for them to have sex. Now.

She unbuttoned his shirt with impatient fingers, crawling up his chest as she leaned down to kiss him. Thoroughly. With open mouth and open passion.

Sweeping his shirt away, she kissed her way down his chest, pausing to circle his flat nipples with her tongue. His body reacted even as his mind shouted to know what the hell was going on with her.

She kissed lower and lower still, unzipping his fly and freeing him. Stroking. Inching closer until her mouth closed over him and his head dug back into the pillow. Her tongue circled him, her hand working up and down the length of his shaft. His fingers twisted in the sheets as he held back the urge to pulsate to completion.

His heartbeat throbbed in his ears. Sweat beaded on his brow from the restraint of holding back.

She looked up at him through her lashes with a sultry expression. He wanted her to have whatever she needed, whatever would bring them closer, even on an elemental level.

His hands roamed along her shoulders and he lifted her upward before he lost control altogether. Even though it damn near killed him to stop.

He owed her the honesty he'd planned for the New Year. Except he couldn't seem to dismiss the knowledge that she hadn't been honest with him for their entire marriage, and about such an important part of her past.

A huge, daunting piece of her. Obviously, the fact that she'd battled through that nightmare of a relationship didn't change how he felt about her. But he worried what it suggested she felt about him that she'd withheld the truth.

"Alaina—"

She tapped his lips before sweeping off her nightgown. "Don't even try to talk me out of this. I know what I want. I know what I need. You. Now."

The sight of her naked other than her panties stunned him silent and made him burn to have her. Only her words stopped him short.

Did she sense that they were headed for trouble once she remembered? Did she know on some subconscious level that memories of their marriage were not all good? Is that why she wanted this moment before their future was taken away?

And then he realized he couldn't do this. Not this way, with so many secrets between them. He couldn't make love to her again until they had more level ground between them. She deserved better from him.

She'd been hurt enough. He couldn't undo his past deceptions. But he could start fresh now and be the man she deserved.

He scooped up her nightgown, the silky fabric still warm from her body. He resisted the urge to press the nightie to his face and take in the scent of her.

Porter cleared his throat and tossed the gown onto the bed. "Alaina, this may be the right time for you, but it's not the right time for me."

She angled up and stared down at him, horror on her face. "Did what I told you about Douglas turn you off?"

Guilt kicked him. How could she think that?

He hated that she'd entertained that thought for even an instant.

Sexy as hell, she was all defiance and challenge, inventing obstacles when they needed to talk. Really talk.

"No, I don't think that. Not at all." He sat up and wrapped a sheet around her. "I want you so much my teeth hurt. But, now that you're having these nightmares and flashes of memories, I wonder if we should be careful." His mind was racing with—hell, he didn't know what exactly. He just felt unsettled. "What if all of this is too much for you, stirring up too many emotions too fast, upsetting you. Maybe we should talk to the doctor again about working on helping you recover your memory."

She bowed her head, eyes averted. "Do you see me as flawed?"

The defiance slid away, leaving behind a vulnerability that rocked him.

He touched her chin, tipping her face so she could see the truth in his eyes. "Don't put words in my mouth. I care about you. I want what's best for you."

"Care? You *care* about me," she hissed, stepping backward. "Be honest with me, Porter. Did we love each other?"

They did. So much. And yet still, he'd lost her. They'd decided to divorce, only reconciling temporarily for the baby.

"Then what's stopping you now? I don't understand."

Of course she didn't because he was holding back so damn much from her. He kept their past a secret out of fear of destroying this new peace between them, this chance to rediscover what they'd had.

The thought of losing her again shredded what was left of his restraint. "Nothing's stopping me." Not tonight. "Absolutely nothing."

He angled forward to kiss her and her purr of approval vibrated up her throat. Things were so right here between them. If only the outside world and concerns—and memories—didn't lurk just outside that door.

For now, he would have her, take and give all he could, hope that she would feel and understand how much she meant to him. He rolled her to her back on the bed, the mattress giving beneath them. With sure but swift hands, he swept off the rest of his clothes and her panties, his urgency sending them fluttering to the floor.

Her milky white skin glowed in the moonlight beaming through the window. She took his breath away.

"Alaina, I could never see you as anything but beautiful, magnificent. Mesmerizing. You take my breath away now every bit as much as you did then. I want you, Alaina, every single day, every minute since I met you, I have wanted you."

When they'd first been married, he'd taken his time learning every curve of her, every freckle and dimple. They'd both talked of being made for each other. How had he lost sight of that?

Almost lost her?

He stretched out over his wife. Flesh to flesh. Truly becoming one as he slid inside her. Moved within her. The warm clamp of her body around him made his heart hammer harder in his chest,

Framing her face in his hands, he kissed her, openmouthed, tongues mating, as well. He couldn't be close enough to her. Wanted more. He wanted forever. The reality of that exploded inside him, filling every corner. It wasn't just about making a family or being parents together. This was about being her husband, her lover, her love.

His feelings for her were more intense than before, steeled by the challenges they faced. He wouldn't take her or what they had for granted.

He loved her.

Three simple words that unleashed everything inside him, sending him over the edge into throbbing release as her cries of completion breathed over his ear. Her fingernails dug into his back as if she ached to stay anchored in this moment every bit as much as he did.

Forever.

His forehead fell to rest on her shoulder and he inhaled the sweet sultry scent of her mixed with an air of their perspiration mingling. The perfume of them together.

Wrapping his arms around her, he tucked her to him and slid onto his side. Her cheek pressed against his chest and she trailed her fingers along his stomach. The ceiling fan spun lazy circles overhead, cooling the air around them.

Reminding him the outside world and concerns couldn't be kept at bay forever. At any moment, she could remember. His time was running out. And even if it wasn't, he owed her the best he had to offer in all aspects of their life together.

"Porter, you never answered my question."

He searched his passion-fogged brain for exactly what she meant. "Which question?"

She raised up on one elbow to look into his eyes. "Did we love each other before I lost my memory?"

He weighed his answer carefully, because yes, he had loved her, so very much. But their past hadn't been as simple as that, and he owed her a more honest future. And he would give it to her.

Still, he needed to be careful not to put too much stress on her, especially so early in her recovery. The nightmares made it clear how her feelings were in turmoil. She was a strong woman, but she'd been through so much. So he would tread warily, step back, figure out and plan the best way and time to tell her.

For now, he had a question to answer. Did they love each other before she'd lost her memory?

He couldn't be sure how she felt at the end, but he'd loved her. Did he still?

God help him, could he love a woman who didn't even remember the first time they met? A woman who didn't know him well enough to love him and might never love him again?

Alaina's frustration level was through the roof. Porter had become distant, and was spending more and more time in his study.

Where was the tender lover? The attentive father?

Between the nightmares and being rejected by Porter, her brain was spinning.

Her life had been frustrating every day since she'd woken from the coma with five years of her life missing, but Porter had counseled her to be patient, all the while romancing her to restore their marriage.

And when she needed romance he shut her out.

Now it was only two days away from Christmas and she couldn't recall ever feeling less in the holiday spirit. How unfair to Thomas. This was his first Christmas. He deserved a house full of love and happiness.

Knotting the belt on her bathrobe, she walked down the quiet hall toward the nursery, the scent of pine from the tree filling the whole giant house. She needed to be near her son and soak up his sweet innocence. To find the peace of rocking him in her arms. And maybe she needed to cry.

Silently nudging the door open, she tiptoed into the room. Her son still slept, his chest rising and falling evenly as he sucked on his tiny fist. Needing the comfort of being close to him, she turned to settle into the rocker.

And stopped short.

Courtney slept on the daybed, a baby bottle of water and powdered formula on the end table. Her arm draped over the side. Why hadn't she noticed before now how much Porter looked like his mother?

Perhaps Alaina made a noise because her mother-in-law startled awake, yawning. "Oh, wow, I must have fallen asleep. I vow that night nanny has the best job ever."

Alaina laughed softly, chocking back the tears in her throat. "We all love Thomas, and I have to confess I appreciate the help." She mixed the bottle and shook the contents. Thomas would be awake at any moment and he would be hungry. "This has been an, um, unusual foray into motherhood."

"You would have done fine on your own. But I'm glad to be here. I thought, well, I wasn't sure how things would be between you and Porter. So I'm here." She stretched, her silk shirt untucked from her skirt. She reached down to retrieve her Jimmy Choo heels. "And I'm seriously in need of a bathroom and a cup of coffee. Do you need anything from the kitchen?"

"Coffee and a biscotti would be nice. No need to hurry, though," she answered, mulling over what Courtney had just said about being unsure of their marriage.

Or, wait, had she put it a different way… Alaina tried to recall the shifting words in her mind. She was having trouble sorting what was real or remembered, or just an impression.

Kind of like those drawings in her sketchbook—she didn't know which images came from real life and which ones were simple dreams until Porter told her.

Her brain was so rattled. She was such a freaking mess. She just wanted to feel certain about something. Anything. When Thomas made a soft cry, Alaina was only too glad for the reprieve from her thoughts.

She turned off the monitor and lifted him

from the crib; his casted leg hung heavily. Her little boy needed her so much.

A quick diaper change later, she settled into the rocking chair and popped the bottle in his mouth, savoring the simple joy of snuggling him close and feeling his warm weight in her arms. She bent to brush a kiss through his baby-fine hair while his little fingers flexed and curled haphazardly around the bottle.

So precious.

More than anything she wanted to remember the day she and Porter had first met Thomas, the day they'd picked him up from the hospital. She ached to recall that moment when they'd first become parents to this beautiful boy. She wanted to be grateful for all she had, but she still couldn't shake the feelings of frustration for all that she'd been denied.

What would happen if she never remembered anything more? Just that thought sent a bolt of panic through her.

Three deep breaths later, she saw her mother-in-law in the doorway with two cups of coffee.

Courtney set one mug down beside Alaina with a small plate of biscotti before sitting elegantly on the edge of the daybed.

"Hmmm." Courtney sighed, holding her mug under her nose and inhaling. "Manna for an exhausted mama."

The java scent wafted from the cup, teasing the air. Alaina's mouth watered but she didn't want to hold the hot drink near her son. "Thank you again for your help caring for him since we brought him home from the hospital."

"Of course I want to help. I'm not the most maternal figure in the world, but we *are* all family." Courtney blew into her mug, then sipped. "I'm just so glad you and Porter have worked things out between you."

Worked things out?

Alaina schooled her face not to show her surprise. Her mother-in-law had let something very telling slip. This was Alaina's chance, the one she'd been waiting for, to unwittingly pry a piece of important information about the past from someone. But getting those words from

Courtney wouldn't be easy. The woman was a savvy lawyer.

Alaina opted to encourage Courtney to finish her thought. "Porter and I have come to an understanding thanks to Thomas."

"Good. I'm so glad the two of you are staying together." She shook her head sadly. "Divorce is tough on children. Although, of course, Porter's father and I were never married, but I think you get my point. It was difficult on my son not having his dad in his life."

Divorce.

There it was. The word she'd feared. The secret Porter had been keeping from her.

They'd been on the brink of splitting up.

Eleven

The family room was still littered with wrapping paper and baby toys. Porter's eyes roved over the chaos, and he couldn't help but smile. It was exactly the way a child's Christmas should be. Presents spread all over the place and a room filled with family. His family.

So far, Thomas's first Christmas had been a success. Porter and Alaina had unwrapped all of Thomas's gifts and taken so many pictures. Even Barry had brought Thomas a gift—a giant puppy stuffed animal that took up a whole couch cushion on its own.

Everything was as it should be. Except for

Alaina's demeanor. That had shifted over the past few days. He could sense her growing frustration. She was angry with him for the time he spent locked away in his office, but it had been all he could do to keep his hands off her while he figured out the best way to tell her he had been holding back important parts of their past. Yes, he'd done so in hopes of rebuilding their family and along the way rediscovered his love for her.

A love that was now in danger again.

If only the doctors could give him concrete answers on her recovery and the odds that painful news could set her back? He knew she was strong. He wanted to trust in what they had.

Except how did a man tell his wife during the holidays that oh, by the way, they'd been talking to lawyers about a divorce shortly before that car accident?

That stark truth didn't fit well into a Christmas bag.

But he wasn't so good at pretending all was well anymore. So when he stepped out of his office, conversation between them had been stiff. Formal.

His mother and her boyfriend had already retired for the evening, leaving Alaina and Porter alone. They'd put Thomas down for the night.

Alaina had begun to stuff a trash bag with the discarded and ripped wrapping paper. She moved with an efficiency and fluidity that radiated anger.

He moved the framed drawing of Thomas she'd given him for Christmas onto the shelf behind the couch. This would be the start of the redecorating process. The process of making this house a home, one that reflected their joint, eclectic tastes.

Assuming he could figure out how best to ease into telling her about their past without destroying their future—while still making sure he didn't somehow harm her recovery.

The radio played through a medley of Christmas songs, filling the space between them. This was his chance. He picked up a neatly wrapped box. He'd given her a ring earlier with Thomas's birthstone, circled with diamonds. But he still had another present for her, something more personal rather than just focused on them as parents, and he'd hoped that in this stolen moment, he would be able to show her how much he cared.

Cared?

He needed to stop using that lukewarm word. He knew he loved her. Deeply. There was no denying that.

The only question? Did his wife still love him?

He tightened the bow on the box and hoped like hell he could get this right with her.

He loved her, more than he could have thought possible.

Her voice halted him. "Were we on the edge of divorce when we adopted Thomas?"

Porter stared at her, unblinking. Heart hammering. "Why would you say that? Do you remember something?"

"Just answer my question." She set aside the bag of discarded wrappings, her posture tense. "Was our marriage over? Were we on the brink of splitting up when I had my accident? Answer me, damn it."

He could feel her anger and her worries even though her voice remained low, her body rigid.

"Our marriage was in jeopardy. Yes. How did you find out?" Were her memories warning her about how close they'd been to throwing it all away? He set aside the package he'd been about to give her.

"Your mother told me." Her tone was flat. Sharp. Accusatory.

He bit back a curse. Why would she do that? Clearly he hadn't told his wife yet and it was his place to share. The betrayal cut deeply. He was disappointed in his mother—and in himself for not handling this better. "I had hoped to wait until after Christmas to tell you, but I see that's only made things worse."

"You're right about that. This can't wait. Not any longer."

"I'm sorry, Alaina, so damn sorry for bungling this. This amnesia… Well, no more excuses. I'm sorry." He thrust a hand through his hair. "The truth is, yes, we planned to get a divorce."

"A divorce," she echoed hollowly. "We were truly on our way to divorce."

"We discussed it with an attorney. But even though we talked about it, we hadn't started official proceedings."

"Why not?" Her eyes flashed with a hint of hope, as if she wanted him to say they'd reconciled.

But he wouldn't lie to her. Not again.

"We'd decided to stay together temporarily, because of Thomas."

"I meant why didn't you tell me sooner, before Christmas week?"

"What good would that have done when you didn't remember? I wasn't supposed to push you—"

"Stop. Just stop the excuses. You misled me. Deliberately." Alaina's eyes narrowed.

"Excuse me for wanting to hold my family together. Yes, I saw it as a chance to repair things so you, Thomas and I could have a future together. Then along the way it became about more. I wanted to romance you. I wanted to win my wife back."

"Win? *Win?*" Her voice rose along with her obvious anger—and hurt. "Win me like I'm some kind of prize?"

Damn, that sounded cold. The truth really did sound better. "Win back your love."

"Marginally better," she conceded, "but still done in a way where you kept me in the dark. You could have said something, done something, to let me know things were more strained than just arguments." Her voice cracked and she paused to take a deep breath. "You know how hard this has been for me, to struggle with not having any memories of you."

Her accusation stung.

"You kept secrets of your own. You never told me what Douglas did to you. We were married, for God's sake. And you never told me." That truth had hurt. But he'd swallowed down the pain in an effort to solidify their future.

"Sounds to me like our marriage was a sham."

She clenched her hands into fists. "I love that child in there, but I don't understand why we chose to adopt if we were about to divorce."

"We weren't about to divorce, damn it."

"Don't quibble. That's the same as lying to me. That stops now." The pain in her voice was audible. "Tell me exactly what happened before I lost my memory. What was the state of our relationship?"

The frustration and agony of those days were indelibly etched in his mind. He paced restlessly, but there was no escaping the past—or the present. "We'd been waiting for a child for a long while. Then right when we'd given up hope on each other, we got the call about Thomas. It was the wrong time, but he needed us. The surgery. We were afraid he would go into the foster system. So we agreed to stay together until the adoption became final."

"And you didn't think this was important for me to know?" Her arms crossed over her chest. Closing him out. Shutting him out.

"You were in no shape—"

"So you decided to climb into my bed again?"

"I wanted to put my family back together. I wanted to win you back and I saw the chance." He stopped his restless pacing and rested his hands on her shoulders. How could he make her see how far he'd come? How much he'd changed? That he wanted this second chance to work between them, not just for their family, but because he loved her.

"The chance to get your way." She shrugged off his hands. "Forget it. Forget everything. This hurts, Porter. This betrayal hurts too much for me to forgive."

Alaina rocked her baby. The nursery provided her with a calming reassurance. She belonged here with him and her heart swelled in pain at the idea of not having this part of her life. Despite the mess of the past few weeks, she knew that a family was all she'd really ever wanted. The time in the nursery with her son was healing to her soul.

Such a precious child. Hers.

And Porter's.

Thomas yawned in her arms, blinking up at her, eyes heavy with sleep.

"Thomas, you know I'll always love you. Always." Her murmur mixed into the gentle lullaby music playing from the mobile over the crib.

She shook her head, still trying to piece together the latest revelation.

Surveying the mural on the wall—the one she'd painted—fuzzy images wafted in and out of her mind. Visits to doctor's offices and specialists. Vacations and hotel rooms. Snippets of a past half remembered, feeling a bit like a dream upon waking.

For a moment, she held her breath, almost afraid breathing would chase the memories away. But instead, the thoughts became clearer, more vivid. Pieces of her past five years began to materialize and to make sense.

And then something else entered her mind that left her stomach in knots.

With a clarity that frightened her, she remembered the car ride home after picking up Thomas. Things had been so strained in the last few months leading up to the adoption. And their inability to conceive had dredged up old memories. Memories of Douglas and the attack and what might have been if he'd never beat her senseless. All of that had come crashing back at her when they'd picked up Thomas and she'd had an all-consuming headache. The pain had only grown worse when she'd realized their son had reminded her of her past. The past she'd been running and hiding from.

A past she'd hidden from Porter. A man she had married and had loved.

A man she loved still.

Porter was on the hunt, storming through the house looking for his mother. He needed to talk to her. To figure out why she'd jeopardized his second chance with Alaina.

He found her in the kitchen, scooping out heaps of mint-chocolate-chip ice cream into a silver bowl embellished with mistletoe.

"Mother, what the hell were you doing?"

"What are you talking about?" She piled more ice cream into the bowl, staring coolly at him.

"You told Alaina that we were getting a divorce."

Courtney's face was impassive. She shrugged nonchalantly. "I told her the truth. Somebody needed to."

"That was my place." Leaning against the counter, he crossed his arms over his chest. He felt betrayed. It wasn't his mother's place to tell Alaina anything about their marriage. Porter inhaled deeply.

"So one would think. Too bad you didn't bother to give her that courtesy before you climbed back into bed with her." She fixed him with an unflinching gaze. The one she was famous for in the courtroom.

"That's really none of your business. I'm acting on the advice of her doctors, trying to ease her memory back."

As she shook her head dismissively, a tight grin spread across her face, not reaching her eyes. "You're using that as a cop-out so you can pursue her."

"I want my wife back. What's the problem with that?"

"The problem is the way you're going about it. I love you, son, but I also love Alaina. And no woman deserves to be tricked by a man who is supposed to love her."

She turned and walked away.

Tricked?

He wanted to call her back. To demand that she listen. He wasn't trying to fool anyone; he'd simply been trying to buy some time to get his family in order. He was simply trying to make Alaina fall in love with him again so she would love him as much as he loved her.

Love?

Yes, he loved her. Just because he hadn't said the words didn't make them any less true.

So why hadn't he thought to tell her?

Now that her initial shock had eased, Alaina wanted to do something to fix the rift between her and Porter. She didn't know exactly how much could be repaired, but she couldn't leave things this way. The only question was where to start. She took a deep breath of the salt air, watching the lights on the yachts twinkle in the twilight, remembering her time on *their* yacht.

She tugged her gaze back to her drawing pad, needing the comfort of her art now more than ever. Sketching a whimsical family portrait—a dream really—she whipped the charcoal across the pad. Pushing with her left foot, she rocked the hammock back and forth. An idea would come to her if she sat here long enough, she was sure of it.

Her brow furrowed as she ran through potential ways to start her conversation with Porter. To make him understand what she'd learned about herself since the accident. About her feelings for him.

If only she could voice her feelings with words as easily as they flowed from her fingertips onto paper—the three of them on their yacht in a tropical locale with a baby palm tree for a Christmas tree and toddler Thomas playing with a new toy boat. She had faith in them as a family. Faith that they could build a future with or without all her memories.

She had her faith in what she wanted from the future.

The sound of shoes shuffling on the ground drew her attention back to the present. Eyes focusing, she saw Porter approaching, a box with glittering gold wrapping paper in hand.

Cocking her head to the side, she peered sideways at him. "What do you have there? You already gave me a gift." She held up her hand with the ring featuring Thomas's birthstone circled by diamonds." The setting was a delicate band of filigree that looked handcrafted.

"I have something else for you. Do you mind if I sit with you?"

She swung her feet off the side of the hammock. "Please."

He lowered himself to sit beside her, his strong shoulder brushing hers and reminding her of the physical chemistry they'd always shared, the heightened awareness she'd always felt around him.

She knew that because she remembered it now.

Wordlessly, he passed her the large gold box. She opened it to find—a binder full of house designs.

"I thought you would want to choose a new house yourself rather than having me assume I know what you want. I would like for us to live in that house together, but that's up to you."

Words failed her. His gift touched her, deep in her soul. She tore her eyes away from the drawings and sketches to meet his gaze, still stunned silent.

"Alaina, I apologize for not being up-front with you from the start."

"I'm the one who owes you an apology." She sighed deeply.

"I'm not sure what you mean."

Bracing for the talk they needed to have, she told herself that honesty and communication were their only hope at this point. That was how they'd patch things together. And it started now.

"I think I lost my memory before the accident," she admitted, although she wanted to see a specialist to discuss it. "I think it had something to do with being afraid to be a parent, being afraid of what happened to me with Douglas."

"I'll never let him near you again." Porter made it sound so simple, but her fears were far more jumbled than that. She didn't fear Douglas coming after her. She feared the wreck of a woman the attack had left behind.

"I realize he's back in jail. I should have told you years ago about what happened and I didn't. I'm in no position to judge you for holding things back. I think I spent so long telling myself that I would be okay, I forgot to show you the weakness behind the mask." Maybe she had hoped that if she forgot about it, that if she never brought it into their relationship, that would be almost the same as if it had never happened.

After her struggle with amnesia, she knew the brain had its own complicated coping mechanisms.

"Seems to me we both have issues with trust." He brushed a hand along her hair, a light caress she wanted to lean into. "What about now that you remember?" Even in the dying light, she could read the worry and fear sparking in his eyes. She was starting to realize just how afraid he was of losing her, of them drifting away from each other.

"I don't remember, not everything. Just snippets about the day of the accident."

"I assumed you remembered…" He rested his head against hers. "My mother said you deserve better from me, better than me. And God, Alaina, she's right. I should have handled everything differently from the moment you woke up in the hospital, from before then, actually."

The bits of Porter she remembered from before the accident would have never said something so tender or allowed himself to be so vulnerable. She recalled how locked in he'd been on the goal of building the family and life he'd thought they should have. She glanced at his gifts—the choices for house plans, the understated but heartfelt ring. These were the gifts of the man she had sensed he might become.

A man she could build her life with.

"I trust you. If you say you love me, then you do."

"But I haven't said it."

"Yet. You will." A smile spread across her lips as she reached for him, fingers twining with his.

"Confident, are you?"

"I'm learning to trust my feelings rather than rely on some black-and-white memory of the past. Feelings, emotions…love…well, that comes in layers and textures that defy simple images."

"Love, you say?" He moved closer. "You love me?"

"I'm still waiting for you to say the words first."

He squeezed her hand tight. Brought his lips to her fingertips and kissed her gently. Butter-flies stirred in her stomach.

His mouth brushed hers again. "Then by all means, I'm more than ready. Alaina Rutger, you are the one and only woman for me, the love of my life, the mother of my child. My partner. My lover. My life."

She took his face in her hands. "Porter, my

love, my partner, father of my child. You are my soul mate for all time even if our minds and memories fade." And she meant it. Every syllable.

Porter dropped to one knee. "Will you marry me?"

"But we're already married." Her eyes widened in a mixture of disbelief and excitement.

"You'll get your memory back someday. I'm confident of that. But even if you don't, I would like for us both to remember the day, the vows." The starlight and Christmas lights caught in his eyes, making them dance with the promise of family and love.

"I adore that plan. I adore you. Yes. Let's get married all over again."

"Renew our vows on New Year's at our Tallahassee house?"

"Perfection." She kissed him deeply. So sure of him. Of them. Of what they could accomplish together as a team.

He pulled away to whisper in her ear. "Yes, you are perfect, Alaina. Absolutely perfect."

Epilogue

One Year Later

"Merry Christmas, my love," Porter said, kissing his wife, the sun warm on his shoulders as they lounged on the upper deck of their yacht.

"Merry Christmas to you, too." She slid from her lounge chair to his, curling up beside him with a happy sigh. "This has been the most amazing family Christmas ever."

Their son napped in his cabin with his grandmother and her new husband keeping watch. Who would have thought Barry would be a keeper? But his mom was happy.

And so was Porter.

He stroked down his wife's arm, linking fingers with her. "I'm glad you found a way to enjoy the yacht."

"Trips together have been a fun escape—" she squeezed his hand back "—and a chance to grow closer as a family."

Waves slapped the side of the craft, chimes singing on their Christmas palm tree. He never would have believed this possible before her accident. But then, he hadn't bought the yacht with the intent of traveling. He'd missed the whole point of a vacation home and the boat, a symbol for his bigger problem.

Life was meant to be enjoyed.

And this past year he'd enjoyed his life more than he could ever remember doing, thanks to his fresh start with Alaina and Thomas.

He stroked a loose strand of blond hair behind her ear. "So you never told me. Why did you choose the Florida Keys for Christmas?"

She tapped her temple. "A week with minimal contact from the outside world?" She grinned.

"What's not to love? I have my husband and son, my family, for the holidays."

Thomas was out of a cast for now, due for another surgery later, but free to crawl around in the sand. He would be a late walker because of his clubfoot, but the doctors expected a full recovery. He was a gloriously healthy child.

They had everything in their life that mattered.

It hadn't always been easy. But they worked at it, finding new paths to make their marriage thrive.

They played this game of surprise often. Her memory had never returned fully, so Porter had suggested she make choices and surprise him. Some small things like dinner dates or larger plans like vacations.

He soaked up the feeling of her skin against his, her bikini leaving a delicious amount of flesh for him to explore with his eyes and hands. "I enjoy your choices for vacations."

"And I appreciate the way you've worked to help me feel more in control of my world. I wish I could have regained all of those missing years, but I'm beginning to accept that may never happen."

He searched her eyes for signs of the pain she'd experienced last year as she began to accept that her memory might not ever come back. She'd remembered good moments and some arguments they'd had, as well. He'd asked to hear every one of them, and as he'd listened, it had helped him hear her side of things. Helped them cement the bond they'd found after the accident.

They had made peace with that past and grown individually, as a couple, too.

He kissed her on her pink nose. "You still haven't fully answered my question. Why the Keys? There are plenty of places for isolation."

She sat up and pulled a box from under her lounge chair. "Why don't you pull the wrapping from your gift and see. That's why I asked you to come up here."

She passed him a two-foot square box with a huge red bow.

They'd already exchanged presents earlier and

one of his had a note inside promising his "special" gift would be given later on the top deck. He'd assumed she meant sex.

This was another surprise.

He tore the large red ribbon from the gift box, lifted the lid. A framed sketch rested inside a satin lining. The charcoal image showed a family of three on their yacht in a tropical locale with a baby palm tree for a Christmas tree and toddler Thomas playing with a new toy boat.

She rested her hand on his elbow. "I was drawing that a year ago when you found me in the hammock and told me you love me. This," she said, tapping the edge of the gift, "was my dream for our family. My hope. And now it's our reality."

"It is, isn't it?"

"The very best Christmas gift ever and I get to enjoy it year-round." Her smile was brighter than the noonday sun. "Thank you."

He traced her mouth and winked. "I guess that means I should cancel our flight out of Miami to Paris."

Laughing, she kissed him, her palms flat against his chest. "Don't you dare. I can't wait to go to the Louvre."

She'd seen the photos of their first trip, one she'd forgotten. Seeing the frustration on her face over that lost moment, he'd known right away what to get her for Christmas.

He set aside the incredible sketch, a treasure for his office, and gathered his wife into his arms to make love. They would experience Paris all over again for New Year's. Some couples didn't get second chances at forever.

He was grateful for every minute of this second chance with Alaina. Each day a beautiful surprise with the love of his life.

* * * * *

MILLS & BOON®

Why shop at millsandboon.co.uk?

Each year, thousands of romance readers find their perfect read at millsandboon.co.uk. That's because we're passionate about bringing you the very best romantic fiction. Here are some of the advantages of shopping at www.millsandboon.co.uk:

* **Get new books first**—you'll be able to buy your favourite books one month before they hit the shops

* **Get exclusive discounts**—you'll also be able to buy our specially created monthly collections, with up to 50% off the RRP

* **Find your favourite authors**—latest news, interviews and new releases for all your favourite authors and series on our website, plus ideas for what to try next

* **Join in**—once you've bought your favourite books, don't forget to register with us to rate, review and join in the discussions

Visit **www.millsandboon.co.uk**
for all this and more today!